THE
SEA ISLANDERS

THE
SEA ISLANDERS

written and illustrated by
JOYCE WEST

SCHOLASTIC BOOK SERVICES
NEW YORK · TORONTO · LONDON · AUCKLAND · SYDNEY · TOKYO

© Text and illustrations, Joyce West, 1970. This edition is pub-
lished by the International Division of Scholastic Magazines, Inc.,
by arrangement with Roy Publishers, Inc. and J. M. Dent & Sons
Ltd.

First Printing .... December 1974

Chapter 1

'In this dilemma . . . I was very pensive.'
from *Robinson Crusoe*, by Daniel Defoe

'It's the police!' Jo hissed. 'She said she was going to ring up the police!'

The four children peered from the first-floor bedroom window of the boarding-house. There was a black police car in the road below.

'Don't be silly!' Miles said, scowling. Miles always scowled when he was frightened. 'They only send for the police when you've done something wrong. We haven't done anything wrong!'

'It's because we're vagrants!' Jo whispered, her eyes very round and her face pale. 'That's what they call it in the papers. No home and no visible means of support. Then the police come and take you up and put you in jail!'

'They don't put children in jail!' Miles said angrily.

'In a *home*!' Jo insisted. 'That's what she said—I heard her. "I'm not going to be left with four kids on my hands," she said. "I'm going to ring up the police about them, they'll have to go to a home!"'

'Nobody's going to send us to a home,' Callie said after a minute in a surprisingly calm voice. She was the eldest, a rather thin girl with straight dark hair and a dreamy manner. Mostly the others listened very little to Callie; they always talked twice as much and twice as loudly as she did. 'We've paid our bill, we can just take our things and walk out and go down to the bus depot.'

They looked at each other for a minute.

'There is a back way,' Miles suggested. 'That sort of fire-escape thing comes out in the back yard and that's on the other street. . . .'

A sort of panic came upon the four of them and they threw the last of their things into the suitcases. Miles sat on the lid of Jo's to make the lock snap. They snatched up their coats and Callie took Rory by the hand. She had to almost drag him because he thought that he had left his mouth-organ under the bed.

The fire-escape was an iron staircase running from the window at the end of the hall beside their bedrooms to the ground. Miles pushed the window open carefully, and one by one the four children clambered through. Callie held tightly to the back of Rory's shirt. There was nobody in the yard and the gate stood open to the back street. Suddenly the children began to run, their suitcases bumping their legs.

'There's a taxi!' Miles cried breathlessly.

In a panic Callie waved her arm; for a moment she thought that the driver had failed to see them, and then the big car slowed down and pulled over to the kerb ahead of them. The driver leaned back and opened the door; they pushed their suitcases inside and tumbled in after them.

'Where to?' said the driver.

'Oh . . .' said Callie. 'To . . . to the bus depot, please, wherever it is that the buses leave for Whangarei.'

The car pulled away, and they sat and looked at one another.

'What are we going to do about the reserved seats to Wellington?' Jo asked in a whisper.

'We'd better not do anything at all,' Callie decided after a minute. 'We'll just buy tickets to Whangarei instead. And we won't give our names; we'll call ourselves something else.'

'Smith?' Jo suggested, brightening up.

'Not Smith,' Miles objected. 'People in books always call themselves Smith when they're trying to hide.'

'Brown . . .?' Jo queried.

'Taylor,' Callie said firmly. 'We're the Taylors.'

It was strange about Callie: usually she took a long time to make up her mind about anything.

'What an awful lot of buses!' Jo said, looking frightened again. 'How are we ever to know which one to get on?'

'They all have their names in front,' Miles told her.

For some reason they were all tiptoeing when they went into the booking-office. Callie went up to the counter to wait her turn.

'Please,' she said, 'can you tell me when the next bus leaves for Whangarei?'

'Ten minutes,' said the man behind the counter, 'and booked out. Sorry. You'll have to wait until this afternoon.'

It was a blow that none of them had expected. Callie swallowed hard. She heard Jo catch her breath with dismay.

'Are . . . are you sure?' she heard herself say. 'I mean that there's no room at all? Because . . . some friends are

3

coming in to meet us at Whangarei . . . they'll expect us.'

It was the first straight-out lie she had told, and her voice shook with nervousness.

'How many?' said the man behind the counter rather abruptly.

'Four,' Callie confessed, 'but one is only very little.'

A man in a grey coat and peaked cap pushed his way up to the counter. He was carrying a clip of papers.

'Two cancellations out there,' he announced. 'Whangarei bus. Changed their minds.'

'Take these kids?' said the booking-clerk. 'Four of them. Squeeze them in?'

'Oh, I suppose so,' the driver allowed.

The booking-clerk clipped out their tickets. 'You'll have to hurry. What's your name?'

'Taylor.'

'Second bus across the street there,' the driver told the children, and they lugged their suitcases back through the traffic, Callie clutching tight to Rory's hand. The driver followed them in a few seconds, and he slung the suitcases into the luggage compartment, clipped the tickets and gave them back to Callie.

'Straight through to the back seat,' he told the children. 'You'll have to squeeze in there somehow.'

The back seat ran right across the width of the bus. In one corner sat an old Maori man, half asleep already, his hands clasped on his stick and his chin resting on his hands. The children had the rest of the seat to themselves, and they rolled up their coats and put them on the rack. Rory insisted upon taking his mouth-organ out of his pocket.

'You're not to play it,' Miles warned him.

'Look!' Jo hissed.

They all looked out of the window, and saw a tall

policeman in uniform getting out of a black car. Another man sat at the wheel.

'Keep your heads down!' Callie whispered fiercely, and they all bent over. Miles pushed Rory's mouth-organ along the seat and they pretended to be looking at it. Callie could feel her heart thumping.

'Where's the driver?' Jo begged in a frightened whisper. 'What's the time? Why don't we go?'

The driver was half way to his seat, but he stopped suddenly, turned around and got out again to take a parcel from somebody.

'Why doesn't he hurry?' Miles muttered.

The tall policeman had gone into the booking-office.

The driver put the parcel down by his own seat and started the engine, and then took up his clip of papers and began checking down a long list. Callie lifted her head enough to see the booking-office door. The tall policeman had just stepped out of it when the driver put down his papers, pushed his cap to the back of his head and did something with the gears. The bus began to move.

In an instant the stream of hurrying traffic had closed in all around. The children sat up in their seats and drew long breaths of relief. Jo looked quite green. Rory announced that he was hungry.

'Of course,' Miles said very low, and looking much brighter, 'I don't suppose for a minute that he was looking for *us*.'

'Can I play my mouth-organ now?' Rory asked.

'No!' said Miles. 'Not in the bus *at all*!'

Callie shut her eyes and leaned back in her corner of the seat. Too much had happened in too short a time.

Chapter 2

'I was born . . . of a good family.'
from *Robinson Crusoe*, by Daniel Defoe

It had all begun with a telegram for John Eliot which had said: 'Can you leave for Antarctic December seventeenth for eight weeks?' They were living at Wairakei then, near Taupo; it seemed to Callie they had never lived long in any one place. John Eliot worked for the Government, for the Department of Scientific and Industrial Research. 'Something to do with earthquakes,' the young Eliots always said in a very vague way when anybody asked them about their father's work.

They had a housekeeper whom they called Mrs Mac. They always had housekeepers because their mother had died when Rory was very young. Rory was five now, the baby of the family; he came quite a way behind Jo and Miles, who were twins. Jo had been christened Joanna, and Callie was Caroline, the eldest. She was not a very good elder sister, she sometimes thought sadly; she hated bossing the younger ones and keeping peace; she was

6

much happier living in some dream world of her own.

There was only a week in which to arrange everything, but at first it seemed easy. Another man was being sent to take over John Eliot's work while he was away, and he and his family would live in the Eliot house. Mrs Mac and the children would go for the school holidays and the extra two weeks to her son's farm on the coast near Auckland. Great-aunt Irene in Wellington wanted the children, but John Eliot felt it would be too tiring for her, and Mrs Mac had suggested the farm. The children were delighted, because Aunt Irene was old and fussy, and Mrs Mac said the farm was by the sea. The three older ones remembered when they had always spent their holidays by the sea.

The children were wildly excited the morning they started out. Their father was driving them to Auckland, and to the farm; he was due to leave late that night by plane from Auckland for Christchurch.

'You can each choose some treat for this afternoon,' he told them.

'Oh, goody!' said Jo. 'Can we have dinner in some elegant place?'

'*Robinson Crusoe*,' Miles decided. 'It's on at the cinema.'

'I want a mouth-organ,' Rory announced, and they all laughed.

'Callie?' John Eliot said. 'Mrs Mac?'

'Dinner at a restaurant will be a very nice treat for me,' Mrs Mac said.

'Callie, wake up!' Miles shouted in her ear. 'What do you want?'

'I want to see a dolphin,' Callie said dreamily.

They all laughed so much that Callie turned pink.

7

'It's this book about dolphins she's been reading,' Jo explained, apologizing for her. She added loyally: 'I'd like to see a dolphin too.'

'Where do you see dolphins?' her father begged of Mrs Mac. 'Do they keep them at the zoo?'

Even without dolphins, it was still a very exciting afternoon. After the cinema, their minds still a delightful haze of lonely beaches and shipwrecks and parrots, they met their father, and he drove them to a fashionable restaurant where he told them they might order what they chose.

'Can we really have anything we like?' Jo breathed.

'So long as it isn't too indigestible,' Mrs Mac said.

'Oh, let them have indigestion just this once,' their father said.

He sighed, but only Callie noticed it. Not many fathers, she thought with a rush of pride, were like theirs, who, no matter how busy he was, still liked to have his children with him. Eight weeks was a very long time, she thought forlornly, and not even letters, probably, as there would have been if he had been going to some sensible civilized place. For a few minutes she wished her father had been interested in anything but earthquakes.

'Callie, do wake up,' said Mrs Mac kindly.

Callie blinked at the large glossy sheet of white card which had appeared in front of her. Jo appeared to be equally confused by the menu. Their father came to their rescue.

'Just leave us a little,' he told the waiter easily. 'We'll work out what we want in a few minutes.'

It was a magnificent meal. Nobody, thought Callie, could possibly have indigestion after a dinner like that. They were waiting for the coffee which was to crown the evening when the music suddenly stopped, and the loud-speaker made an announcement.

'Mr John Eliot,' it said. 'Calling Mr John Eliot. Mr Eliot, will you please come to the manager's office.'

The children looked from one to the other, almost frightened, but their father was quite calm.

'Probably some alteration in the time of the flight. I gave them this address.'

He was back in a few minutes.

'Mrs Mac,' he said, putting his hand under her arm, 'could you come for a minute?'

It was all more puzzling than ever. Presently John Eliot came back and sat down on the edge of his chair. He looked very grave, Callie thought.

'That was a cable for Mrs Mac. The Post Office has been trying to get her all day. Her daughter in Edinburgh is very ill, probably dying. I'm afraid you'll have to go to Aunt Irene. I've got a lot of things to do now. I'm going to try and get an air passage for Mrs Mac. I don't know how lucky I'll be, especially at this hour of the night. Then she won't have enough money: I'll have to cash a cheque somewhere. She's talking to her son now.'

They all looked at him blankly. There did not seem to be anything to say.

'You stay here,' he said, 'and have your coffee. Then you can go into the lounge out there and wait for me. I may be a long time, but don't move from there. I'll be back.'

The time seemed endless. They finished their little cups of hot strong coffee, and they went into the lounge and sat in huge soft chairs and turned over the pages of magazines. Rory fell asleep with his mouth-organ in his hand and his head in Callie's lap. The evening dragged on and on.

At last John Eliot came in. He sat down wearily, and they came and stood around him.

'I've got three-quarters of an hour to catch my plane,' he said. 'Everything's fixed up. There was a cancellation, and I got Mrs Mac on the first flight for Sydney. I've sent a telegram to Aunt Irene; she'll be pleased if nobody else is. We'd better go—I've booked you in at a boarding-house in Symonds Street; I've stayed there before. Mrs Green; she'll look after you. And I've booked you for tomorrow on the nine o'clock bus to Wellington. Can you get a taxi and get yourselves down to the bus? Aunt Irene will meet you the other end.'

'Yes, of course,' Callie said as bravely as she could.

It was like a bad dream. They stumbled out of the car in an unknown street, and John Eliot took them to the door and rang the bell. Then he kissed them all, quickly and a little fiercely.

'God knows I hate leaving you like this! Take this money, Callie—be careful of it. Keep out enough for your rooms tomorrow morning and the bus, and put the rest away to give Aunt Irene. Now listen, the rest of you— Callie's boss. You do as she says.'

Next minute he was gone, and they heard the car start up.

The door was opened by a woman who seemed in a great hurry.

'Where is he?' she demanded. 'Where's your father?'

'He's gone,' Callie said.

The woman looked from one to the other of them, and a very unpleasant expression came over her face.

'His telegram came back,' she said, 'not delivered. I

was on the phone when you rang the bell. The Post Office can't deliver the telegram to your aunt, she's been knocked down by a car and she's in hospital. You'd better get your father back.'

'We can't,' Callie said flatly, after a long silence.

The woman called Mrs Green looked at them in a very peculiar way. She was standing between them and the stairs.

'Well, what do you propose doing now?' she wanted to know.

Her tone made Callie straighten her shoulders. 'Callie will look after you,' her father had said.

'Please show us to our rooms now,' she said. 'We shall make up our minds in the morning.'

Once upstairs, nobody had any idea what to do, so they just went to bed. Callie's last conscious thought was that she would not sleep a wink. When she awoke the sun was shining. Jo was awake too; they crept into the boys' room and sat on the floor.

'I want to go home!' Rory said suddenly. He pushed out his lower lip. 'I don't like it here.'

'You know you can't go home,' Jo explained to him, tears springing to her eyes. 'There are people living in our house.'

'Perhaps we could go to Mrs Mac's son, anyway,' Miles suggested.

'He lives on his own,' Jo said dolefully. 'He wouldn't want four children turning up. Anyway, it's his sister that's ill . . .'

'I want to go home!' Rory demanded.

'You can't,' Jo told him, and the tears spilled over and ran down her cheeks. 'We haven't got a home.'

'Oh, shut up!' Miles said. 'You'll make him worse.

Funny, I never noticed it, but we haven't many relations, have we?'

'Father came out from Scotland,' Callie said thoughtfully, 'and Mother was an only child. There's only Aunt Irene, and those cousins away down in the south, at Queenstown or somewhere . . .'

'Do you think they might have us?' Miles suggested.

'What's their name?' Callie asked. 'Does anybody know?'

'I think it's Robertson . . .' Jo said doubtfully.

'Well, there you are,' said Callie. 'We can't set off to spend eight weeks with people we don't even know the name of, don't know where they live and haven't been asked. And the fares would take all our money.'

'I'm hungry,' Rory said.

'So am I,' Jo confessed. 'Shall I go to the stairs and see if anyone is making breakfast?'

She was back in two minutes, her face very pale. She tiptoed in, closed the door and leaned against it.

'You know what she said?' she burst out in a stricken whisper; 'that Mrs Green woman, I mean. I heard her from the stairs . . .'

'*What* did she say?' said Miles when Jo ran out of breath.

'She said: ''*There's something funny going on here.* I don't like the look of it. I'm not going to be left with four kids on my hands. I'm going to ring up the police. If they've got no money and no people they'll have to go to a home!'''

The children sat and looked at one another. Rory came and leaned against Callie's knees.

'Maybe we should have tried to get Father back,' Jo whispered.

Callie was silent, quite pale, lost in concentration.

'What,' she said, 'about Penguin Island?'

It was so long ago that they had almost forgotten Penguin Island, a rocky point of land, not quite an island, somewhere up near the tip of New Zealand. It was mixed up in their minds with memories of their mother, and of blue sea channels and bright sand and summer holidays, the smell of the seaweed and the cries of the oyster-catchers over the shell beds.

For a few moments nobody spoke, but Jo's tears had stopped.

'Are you sure it still belongs to Father?' Miles asked.

'Of course,' Callie said. 'He paid the rates last year, I know. And he told me then he'd never sell it, because it had belonged to Grandfather and we'd been so happy there, and maybe we'd like to go there again some time when we were grown up.'

'Why did we stop going?' Jo asked.

'I think maybe because we were so happy there,' Callie said, rather low. 'I mean with Mother and all. I think Father wouldn't go back without her, and then he got transferred down to Christchurch, remember? And we never went back.'

'*Could* we go there?' Miles demanded.

'How could we go?' Jo asked.

'By bus, I suppose,' Callie said, thinking. 'Get the first Road Services bus that goes to Whangarei, and then find out which bus goes nearest. And then take a taxi, I suppose. Or walk. It would be the only way now we haven't got a boat of our own to take us the shorter way by sea. You remember we used to walk out to the road sometimes and get meat and things off the bus.'

'I remember going through Maori places,' Miles said.

'I remember the sea,' Rory announced.

'Oh, you can't!' Jo told him. 'You were much too small.'

'I do, I do!' Rory shouted, flying into a dreadful passion. 'I do so remember the sea. There was a lot of it! I was not too small!'

'Of course not,' Callie soothed him. 'There was a lot of sea.'

'How much money have we got?' Miles said gruffly.

Callie brought out the little packet her father had given her. There were ten ten-dollar notes folded together and fastened by a rubber band. She had fifty cents of her own, Jo had twenty-five cents, Miles had forty cents in small change and Rory had eight cents.

'You can have my money, Callie,' he said generously.

'First, we must pay our board,' Callie said. 'Then bus fares, and a taxi to take us to the bus, and we don't know how much we will have to spend from Whangarei on. And we have to live for eight weeks until Father gets back . . . we can catch fish, perhaps, but some things we must buy.'

'Do you think we can do it?' Jo asked fearfully.

'Of course we can!' said Miles. 'We'll be just like Robinson Crusoe.'

At that moment the gong banged in the hall below.

'We're not going down to *breakfast*, are we?' Jo demanded, pale.

'Of course we are,' Callie said firmly. 'And you must all eat as much as you possibly can. We'll go down now and pay Mrs Green and let her think we've gone to these Robertson people. I won't actually tell a lie. Come along, we'll go together; she can't eat us.'

She took Rory's hand. They found Mrs Green in the office.

Callie cleared her throat.

'Please could you make up our bill. I'd like to pay you now so that we can get away right after breakfast.'

'Oh, you're going some place, are you?' said Mrs Green. 'And where are you going, may I ask?'

'We have cousins in the South Island,' Callie said calmly. 'Their name is Robertson. There's an early bus to Wellington, so we're in rather a hurry.'

She put down a ten-dollar note in front of Mrs Green, who was beginning to look a little less cross.

'Well, I hope you know what you're doing,' said Mrs Green, pushing back a receipt and a very small amount of change, 'and where you're going, especially with the little boy.'

'Yes, thank you,' said Callie, smiling stiffly. 'We used to live in the South Island, and we're quite used to travelling by ourselves.'

She led the others into the dining-room. They ate porridge, and then bacon and eggs and sausages. While nobody was looking Callie hid some slices of bread under her cardigan. When she was unable to make anybody eat anything more they got up and went upstairs to finish packing.

It was then, looking from the window, that they saw the police car in the street below.

Chapter 3

'Never any young adventurer's misfortunes, I believe, began sooner than mine.'

from *Robinson Crusoe*, by Daniel Defoe

By the time they reached Whangarei the sun was no longer shining.

'I'm hungry,' Rory said.

They had long since eaten the bread which Callie had carried away, and the apples which she had bought when the bus stopped half way.

'How are we going to find out where to go, and which bus to take?' Jo asked, beginning to look frightened again. People were meeting other people; it seemed as if everyone but the Eliots had somewhere to go.

'Ask, of course,' said Miles. He was cross because he too was uncertain.

They asked at the Road Services office, but there was no service there that was much use to them. Their best plan, the man in the office explained, was to go to the depot of Far North buses, two streets away.

'You and Rory had better stay here,' Callie told Jo, 'or take him for a little walk. He's tired of sitting. Don't go far.'

They found that the Far North daily bus left quite soon. Callie had a moment of blind panic when she realized that she did not know exactly where they wanted to go. She and Miles looked helplessly at each other, and the man in the office came to their rescue. He produced a large map and spread it on the counter.

'There!' said Callie with a rush of relief; she laid her finger on the map; the name Awatea Stream had sprung out at her; she remembered it.

'O'Reilly's Corner,' said the man briskly. 'Ask the driver to put you down at O'Reilly's Corner. Leaves in twenty minutes.'

They paid for their seats and hurried back to collect Jo and Rory and the suitcases. Jo came running to meet them; she had been crying and her hair was wild. Rory clutched a small black dripping kitten with a string around its neck.

'Some boys were throwing stones at it!' Jo wept. 'It was in the water and it was drowning!'

'Yes, and Jo throwed stones at the boys!' Rory announced, 'and she said bad words too, and the boys ran away!'

'Please, Callie, give me some money to buy it some fish!'

'I'm hungry too!' Rory said. 'I want some fish and chips.'

It was almost too much for Callie. Miles came to her rescue.

'We'd better all have fish and chips,' he decided. 'We can take them along with us. And a couple of bottles of drink.'

'Look,' Callie said to Jo, 'here's the money, you and Rory go into the shop and ask for sixty cents' worth of fish and chips, and then stand there right by the door till we pick you up. You can open the parcel and give the kitten a bit. Then let it find its way home.'

'It hasn't got a home!' Rory said indignantly.

'Please cut the string off its neck,' Jo said, wiping her eyes with the back of her hand. 'It's nearly choked.'

Miles cut the string and the kitten opened a pink triangular mouth and mewed quietly. Callie was almost in tears herself.

'See?' she said. 'It'll be all right now. Here's the money, and stay by the door. Miles and I are going to carry the suitcases round.'

The bus was waiting by the kerb, a rather small bus with a battered look about it, as if it were accustomed to run into a few rocks or cows on every trip north. It was very dusty. They gave the suitcases to the driver, and Callie climbed into the bus and spread out their coats over two double seats, one behind the other. Miles went back to collect Jo and Rory and the fish. Callie sat on the edge of her seat tense with anxiety for fear he would miss them, or that Jo had rushed off with the kitten somewhere, but all was well. The driver was still busy loading his pile of mail-bags, luggage, newspapers and paper parcels when the three of them appeared, Jo carefully carrying a largish newspaper bundle.

'I'm hungry!' Rory said. He smiled gently at Callie and settled himself into the seat behind. She had a moment of wondering uneasily why he looked so sweet, but she was busy dividing the greaseproof paper into four pieces and sharing out the chips and pieces of fish. She passed two portions back to Rory and Jo, and had a sudden impulse to laugh at the thought of how horrified Mrs Mac would have been. Nobody seemed to be looking at them; two children in the front seat were eating ice-creams, and the old Maori lady across the aisle was opening up a newspaper parcel herself. Even Miles, who was usually so proper, was starting happily on his share of fish and chips.

It was all scalding hot and brown and delicious, and Callie discovered that she was furiously hungry herself. She had stopped worrying. For the next few hours it was no good thinking about anything; she could just sit in the bus. At least they were started in the direction where they wanted to go. The only thing that still troubled her was the thought of the kitten.

'M'mm—this is very nice fish and chips . . .' Rory was murmuring to himself. Callie turned round to see how he was getting on, and she was just in time to see his hand, with a little flake of fish, go inside his shirt front.

Struck with horror, she poked Miles and he turned round. Rory was not looking at them, but Jo was, and the pink colour rose slowly over her face right up to her hair. 'Nice fish and chips,' Rory went on mumbling to himself, lifting a chip to his mouth and, in the opening of his shirt just under his chin, there appeared for a minute long black whiskers and the tip of a tiny triangle of a furry, black face.

Hurriedly he pushed the black face back out of sight and smiled angelically at Callie and Miles, and helped himself to another potato chip.

'Now they'll probably put us off the bus,' Miles muttered as they turned back. 'Why couldn't you have *watched* him?'

'*You* could have watched him,' Callie said crossly. 'Anyway, it's Jo's fault, she's older.'

19

They finished their meal, and Miles brought out his pocket knife and took the tops off the bottles and passed one bottle back to Jo and Rory. At least the kitten was all right, she thought with a sudden wave of relief, but her imagination ran on and she saw a dreadful scene in which the kitten cried and attracted everyone's attention, the bus driver scolded them at the top of his voice, and ended up by insisting that they either throw the kitten out into the road or get off along with it.

Callie suddenly felt she could cope with it no longer, and she put her head down on her rolled-up coat on the window-sill and went to sleep. She slept for a long time, uneasily, rolling over onto Miles's shoulder and waking, rolling back and bumping her head against the side of the window. She dreamed short, uncomfortable dreams in which Rory was lost, she was lost; she travelled for ever and arrived nowhere.

When she finally awoke her neck was stiff. It was late in the afternoon. Miles was staring out of the window, but the other two were asleep. Rory's head was on Jo's shoulder, and he slept with his angelic look on his face. There was a bulge in his shirt front.

When the old Maori lady across the aisle saw Callie looking round she began to laugh, and pointed to the lump that was the kitten.

'He's a very quiet passenger,' she said.

For a moment Callie was worried, and then she saw that the old woman really did think it funny. She laughed too.

'I'm afraid my brother's a very bad boy.'

'Oh no!' the old lady said. 'That's a very nice little boy. Where're you fellows going?'

'We're getting off at O'Reilly's Corner,' Callie told her.

'Eh?' she said. 'O'Reilly's Corner. You don't live there, do you? I've never seen you before.'

'No,' Callie said. 'We've just come for the school holidays.'

She seemed satisfied, and Callie looked out of the window again. After all the long, dull, inland travelling of bush and scrub and farmlands and bush again, they had come out on the sea. Tidal flats stretched away on the one hand, looped by shining channels of water. From the windows on the other side of the bus Callie could see a cove with anchored boats. They crossed a bridge where pohutukawa trees leaned down, unbelievably red. A strip of green with bright tents and parked cars went flickering past.

'A lot of people come here in the holidays,' the old Maori lady told them.

The bus stopped every few miles, and the driver left parcels, put down mail-bags and tossed out rolled-up newspapers. He stopped to give a paper to a man driving cattle, and they talked for a little while, the man on the horse sitting sideways on one hip, one foot out of the stirrup and his reins dangling. They passed three white goats walking slowly, and Maori children bathing, quite naked, under a wooden bridge.

When the bus stopped at a beach store beside a camping ground, the driver said: 'Fifteen minutes break. Get out and stretch your legs.'

'Can we get out?' Rory cried, bouncing up. 'I'm thirsty. Can we have an ice-cream?'

There were not many people left in the bus now, and they all got out. Callie's legs felt stiff from sitting so long.

'Please,' Rory begged, 'can we have ice-creams?'

'I guess we should buy some stuff,' Miles said in a low voice to Callie. 'Bread and butter and all that sort of thing.'

'I guess so,' Callie said, startled. The thought of arriving in an empty house was rather frightening.

She and Miles went into the little store, and she tried to recall what they would need. There were two spare loaves of bread, so she bought them, and a pound of butter, and some cheese and biscuits. Then she decided on a dozen eggs and a tin of jam, and Miles collected tea, sugar and a tin of salt. It seemed to add up to a great deal of money.

'May as well get four ice-creams,' Miles suggested. 'We won't be having ice-creams again for a while.'

Rory and Jo had gone down to the little beach at the water's edge. Rory sat cross-legged and blew his mouth-organ softly, and the kitten scratched with tiny black paws in the sand.

'You've been a very bad boy,' Callie said severely.

'Yes, Callie,' Rory said, smiling angelically. 'Thank you, Callie.'

It was a queer sort of afternoon, very still, and it was a queer beach. Twisted trunks of pohutukawa trees over-hung the sand, and out in the estuary there were tangled mangroves. Under the low, heavy clouds the tide-channels were olive-green, the same colour as the mangroves.

'Come on,' said Callie, 'we'd better get back to the bus.'

It was while they were walking in, past the driver's seat, that the dreadful thing happened. The kitten, pushed back down Rory's shirt-front, gave a piercing miaow. Everyone seemed to turn round and look at the children. Callie, holding her breath, could feel the driver's eyes on Rory.

Only Rory smiled sweetly, and put up his mouth-organ and blew a hideous note.

'That's my mouth-organ,' he told the driver.

The children scurried guiltily back to their seats, and in a minute the bus was on the move again. The country seemed very wild and lonely now, gold hills and dark bush, and waves breaking over wet rocks. The road rolled on, up hill and down again, climbing steep corners, sliding through dark gullies turning and turning upon itself until Callie had the nightmare feeling that they were travelling in circles and would never arrive at their journey's end.

They were almost the last people left when the bus stopped, and the driver looked back over his shoulder.

'This is what they call O'Reilly's Corner. You kids getting off here?'

Callie's heart had begun to thump wildly. She felt that it was impossible that they should leave the safe and comfortable shelter of the bus that had been their home for the last few hours. Her hands shook as she tried to gather their coats and parcels. Jo looked pinched, and Rory's arms were folded defiantly over the bulge in his shirt. Miles began pushing the others down the aisle.

The driver was already getting their suitcases out of the back of the bus.

'You kids be all right here?' he asked. 'It's going to rain. Somebody meeting you?'

'Oh yes, thank you,' Callie said falteringly. It was not quite as hard to tell a lie this time. 'They must be late.'

The driver chucked Rory under the chin and then flicked the lump in his shirt.

'Been a quiet passenger, that one!' he said, grinning, as he climbed back into the bus.

23

The children stood close together, staring after him, and he swung out onto the step again.

'You're sure you're all right?' he asked.

'Oh yes, yes, thank you!' they called after him, and he climbed back in. They heard the gears grind.

As they stood there by the roadside, their suitcases at their feet, and watched the bus disappearing from sight down the dusty road, the first drops of rain began to fall.

Chapter 4

'And now our case was very dismal indeed.'
from *Robinson Crusoe*, by Daniel Defoe

Callie had expected O'Reilly's Corner to be a little township like those through which the bus had passed during the day. She had thought that there would be a store, a post office, certainly a garage where they might hire a taxi to take them the rest of the way.

This was exactly what it said, a corner and nothing more. The road ran three ways into the rain and the hills, and the telephone wires made a low, dismal humming. There was not a building in sight and no sign of life. There were only tall hills, with masses of grey rock, like castles, disappearing into the misty sky above.

A bitter self-reproach seized Callie. She had promised to look after the others and instead, by her reckless decisions, she had brought them to this. She was recalled from her trance of despair by hearing Rory sniff. She took his cold hand.

'Come on,' she said as cheerfully as she could, 'we'll

shelter under that big rock while we decide what to do.'

'Where is Penguin Island?' Jo said in a shaking voice.

Miles shook his head. 'I don't even know which way the sea is.'

They dragged their suitcases across the road verge to the rock. It was huge, curved like a seashell for giants. There were two mail-boxes beside it and a sort of wooden cupboard for parcels. The children sat on their suitcases, huddled together, and Rory sniffled a little.

'I'm hungry,' he said. 'I want to go home. Toby wants to go home too . . . and it's getting dark . . .'

All this, Callie told herself in sick misery, was her fault. Anything would have been better than crouching under a rock in the rain in this queer, wild, lonely countryside.

'It's raining harder,' Jo said.

It was not only raining harder, it was getting dusk. At that very moment of despair Callie heard a sound.

'It's a car!' Miles cried. They could hear it clearly, labouring up the hill, an old-sounding car, chugging noisily along.

'Surely they'll give us a lift,' Callie said desperately, 'or take a message, get us a taxi . . . they couldn't just go past!'

The car came into sight, its dim headlights cutting through the rain and twilight. There was another noise; the people inside were singing loudly. As the headlights picked up the children's figures beside the road, the car wavered to the verge and then wavered back again. It stopped with its engine running noisily.

'Hey!' said the driver.

'Why . . .' Jo breathed in horror, 'they've been *drinking* . . .'

'Hey!' the driver shouted. 'You kids lost or something?'

Rory's cold clutching hand filled Callie with a desperate courage.

'Come on,' she said, 'they can't eat us.'

The men in the car were all Maoris. The reflection from the headlights shone on dark faces and white teeth.

'Where're you kids going?' the driver asked. He was young, curly haired.

'We want to get to Penguin Island,' Callie said in little more than a whisper. 'We got off the bus and now we don't know our way.'

They all leaned out of the car and looked at the children.

'Can't leave 'em here,' said a voice from the back. 'Better take 'em along, eh?'

'You got some bags or something?' the driver asked.

The car appeared to be already more than full, but the suitcases were fitted in somewhere. Callie thought suddenly of Mrs Mac. 'Never, *never* get into a car with a strange man,' she always told the children. Callie began to shake with laughter at the thought of Mrs Mac's face if she could see them getting into a car filled with drunken Maoris. 'I'm hysterical, that's what I am,' she told herself.

'Don't worry,' Miles whispered sturdily. '*I'll* look after you.'

Callie found herself wedged between two stout men with Jo in her lap. Rory rode on the knees of the man next to the driver and nursed his kitten. 'All aboard!' cried the driver, and started with a clash of gears. They turned into the right-angled road and bumped over ruts and stones. All at once it seemed to have grown quite dark. The headlights were dim, rain fell heavily and the metalled surface was so rough that Callie was not sure at what point they left the road and took to the paddocks. She saw ferns and drifts of rushes and the wheels squelched loudly.

'Hey!' somebody yelled. 'Look out for the swamp, you, Horowai! A man would think you're drunk or something!'

Next moment they were stuck. The wheels whirred and paddled. Everyone seemed to think it a joke and piled out into the rain, laughing loudly. 'You stop there,' they said. 'You're not very heavy.'

They all pushed, the engine roared and rattled, the old car began to move again and in a moment everyone was squeezing back again, banging doors and roaring with laughter. They climbed a steep hill and, if Callie had not been too tired to feel anything at all, she would have been terrified, for the old car groaned and laboured so heavily that each moment she expected it to fall to pieces and roll down into the darkness below.

'I guess it's just about time this joker Horowai got himself a new car,' someone said. They must have reached the top, for the car was now lurching quickly downwards, the headlights swaying and turning in the sharp bends of the track. Suddenly they stopped and the doors were flung open. Slowly Callie climbed out into the soft rain and darkness. Everyone was disappearing. There were lights near by and Callie smelled the sea.

'Where's Rory?' she said shakily.

Jo was shivering too. 'That man carried him away . . .'

Miles stood close to them. They heard a woman's voice raised in scolding tones, and then a man appeared in the darkness.

'The old woman says you better come in,' he said sheepishly.

The three children stumbled after him, up some wooden

steps and into a large room lit by two kerosene lanterns. There was a delicious smell of cooking food. In one corner a large wood stove roared away, its top nearly red-hot, and on a rug in front of the fire sat Rory and the black kitten, solemnly warming themselves.

Callie had just time to see all this when they were taken in charge by a little old lady. She was not much taller than Miles, dressed all in black, with a black handkerchief tied over her white hair. Her face was very wrinkled, but her large dark eyes snapped with energy.

'What you doing standing out in the rain?' she demanded of Callie. 'These men got no sense to leave you there. Ai, look at that. Wet!'

In an instant their coats were stripped from them.

'Sit down by the fire,' the old lady ordered. 'Get dry.'

Callie did exactly as she was told. Slow tears of relief stood in her eyes. For the moment they were all warm and safe.

In a very few minutes four plates appeared, laden with boiled potatoes and some sort of delicious-smelling stew. Callie found she was ravenous.

'This is the nicest thing I ever ate,' Miles mumbled.

'It's mussels,' said a girl who was sitting watching.

Callie was trying not to laugh. Mrs Mac would never let them eat shellfish; they were 'not safe', she said. It was impossible to imagine what Mrs Mac would say if she could see all four of them, even Rory, at this hour of the night, devouring large plates of shellfish. To make matters worse, the kitten was lapping with a very dainty tongue from the side of Rory's plate. Everyone seemed to think it a huge joke, and Callie was much too tired to worry.

She found suddenly that someone was talking to her.

'So you're Johnnie Eliot's kids?' the old lady was

29

saying. 'You're going to stop out in that old place? Who'll look after you?'

Somehow Callie felt it would be useless to tell the little old lady anything but the truth. It was a great relief.

'Only for the school holidays. My father had to go away, and my great-aunt, who was going to look after us, had an accident. And I'm going to look after the others.'

Everyone burst into loud laughter. Callie had no idea that she had said anything very funny. The old lady cackled.

'Yes, you keep 'em in order. Well, you've grown a bit, anyway. I remember you, skinny little thing with long hair, all the time with your father. Well, come on, Paul will take you over, tide'll be about right.'

Three men went with them. The curly haired Paul picked up Rory, who had fallen fast asleep. Jo took the kitten. One of the men was carrying blankets. They packed themselves into the old car and Paul started the engine. They bumped over ruts and tussocks, but it was a much more sober journey this time. The car stopped and Paul said: 'Now you got to walk.'

Paul still carried Rory and the other two men took the suitcases. The three children followed with bags and parcels, the blankets and the kitten. It was very dark and the men walked fast; Callie found herself hurrying to keep them in sight, slipping and sliding on the rough track. Presently they were coming downhill again. She could hear the sound of waves.

The men had stopped. 'You want to be careful here,' one said.

Somebody took Callie's hand and led her forward. It was black dark and very misty, and somewhere below she heard the sound of sea on rocks. In a moment Jo joined her, then Miles. The path seemed to broaden.

'All right now,' Paul said.

Soon they reached sand. The rain had stopped, but the night was misty and the air smelled of salt and seaweed.

'You got to walk through the water here,' Paul said. The children took off their shoes; the water was cold, not quite to their knees. They left it behind and stumbled over drifts of sand and seaweed. Some kind of birds called with mournful voices through the darkness. Suddenly Callie realized they had reached the house.

They groped their way up the steps and someone tried the door.

'Better break a window, maybe,' Paul offered.

Strangely, it was Jo who remembered where the key was kept. She kneeled on the lower step and groped back into the space under the veranda boards, and gave a little cry of triumph.

Paul took it from her and opened the door with a squeak of unoiled hinges. He had matches and a candle in his pocket, and he gave a satisfied grunt when he saw that there was wood in the box beside the fireplace. He knelt down and brought out a knife and cut shavings, and in a few minutes there was a small cheerful fire. He laid on more sticks.

'Guess you'll be all right now, eh? You don't want to mind if you hear some funny noises under the house—penguins, maybe.'

'Oh yes,' Callie said, 'I remember them!' She was suddenly shy. 'Thank you very much—you have been very kind to us.'

'She's right,' Paul said. 'Old Lucy, she told us to. We all do what she says.'

They all laughed.

'Mrs Lucy,' said Rory, waking up. 'I like her.'

'Mrs Harakaia,' Paul said, 'that's her name now. She's had three husbands. She's my grandmother.'

'I call her Mrs Lucy,' Rory announced. 'I call my kitten Toby.'

Paul put another log of wood on the fire, and next minute the men had gone and the children were alone.

They were all much too tired to think of looking for beds. Callie pulled the fireguard across the hearth and spread out one of Mrs Lucy's blankets. They rolled up their coats for pillows, lay down in the firelight and pulled up the other two blankets. In a few short minutes they were all asleep.

Chapter 5

'When I waked it was broad day, the weather clear and the storm abated.'
from *Robinson Crusoe*, by Daniel Defoe

Callie woke to the unfamiliar voices of shore birds. It took her a long time to realize what she was doing lying on her back on the floor of a perfectly strange room, staring up at a ceiling covered in cobwebs. Around her neck was curled something warm and furry.

She put up her hand and discovered Rory's kitten and remembered everything. Cautiously she slid out from under the blankets and padded barefoot across the room to open the front door and look out.

It was like throwing wide some magic window that took her back to being a very small child again. Nothing was strange; it was all familiar. The rain was gone, the sky was clear, and there lay the pale brown, crescent-shaped beach of Penguin Island with drifts of drying seaweed. The bright water's edge was like a curving mirror.

She found Jo beside her, and then Miles.

Shags and gulls, Penguin Bay

'Isn't it beautiful?' Jo breathed.

'I'd forgotten how close the house was to the sea,' Miles said. 'Look, nothing but the beach between!'

'Oh yes, and the grass!' Jo cried. 'We used to call it kitten-tails, do you remember? And the little pink convolvulus flowers in the sand . . . but where's the other beach—wasn't there a beach with surf?'

'On the other side of the island,' Callie said, thinking. 'It isn't quite an island, you know, just a long point. It's cut off at high tide; you know, where we walked through the water last night. This side is the estuary side, where the Awatea river comes out; the ocean is over the hill.'

Miles was looking back towards the rocky hills of the mainland.

'That's where we came down last night . . . see the track? It's the only way you can get here, except by boat. It really is like Robinson Crusoe's island, isn't it? A real sea island all to ourselves!'

Rory had wakened and he came and looked out, pushing between them.

'It's the sea,' he said. 'I told you it was here.'

All of a sudden he let out a loud yelp and went galloping down the steps and across the sand, screaming with pleasure. The kitten scampered after him, whisking up a tiny sandstorm. Callie felt herself running too, Miles and Jo in pursuit. She felt quite light-headed with the smell of the sea and the brightness of the morning light, with relief from anxiety, and the heady sense of eight long weeks of freedom ahead.

'It's nasty to run away from me!' Rory scolded, coming panting up with the kitten to where the others had thrown themselves into a sand drift.

'Isn't it a little house?' Jo said, looking back along the beach.

From where the children lay it was a very little house, low and silvery, half buried in the sand and sea-grass. Callie felt it was not quite like any house she had ever known before. Most places were built of materials carried to the spot, of brick and cement and dressed timber: the house at Penguin Island looked as if it had grown up out of the beach and was a part of it; the little blue penguins nested beneath it, spring tides came up to the doorstep and sea-birds flew overhead.

'I'm hungry!' Rory said.

'So am I!' Jo said, alarmed. 'What are we going to eat?'

The house at Penguin Bay

'There's plenty to eat,' Callie reassured them. 'We'll light the fire and make toast and have an egg each. Only just for this morning—we won't be able to afford eggs for breakfast every day.'

'It won't matter,' Miles told her. 'I'm going to catch fish. There's a boat in the shed, maybe we can go out fishing.'

'Not in the boat, we can't,' Callie said. 'It's got holes in it, it would sink. And look. If we're going to live here by ourselves there's work we've got to do. We can fish and swim later. We'll go back and get breakfast and then we'll have to clean the place out, sweep away the sand and spiders' webs, and put out mattresses and so on to

36

air. And find out exactly what we've got in the house.'

To her relief, Miles agreed.

'Come on, you two,' he ordered Jo and Rory, 'pick up some of the wood and we'll take it back.'

'Maybe', he said to Callie when they got back, 'we should divide our money up into eight weeks, and then we'll know what we can use.'

Callie thought it over.

'Suppose we take out something first. Ten dollars, say. In case someone got sick or we might need something. Then we can use the rest.'

The others agreed, and Callie hid the money carefully under a loose board below the window-sill. From the suitcase she found old shorts and shirts for everybody, and they set to work.

There were two bedrooms, one behind the other, at the side of the big living-room, and a lean-to kitchen behind, placed so that the one chimney served the open hearth in the living-room and the kitchen stove. The house was shaped like a square box, with another, smaller box behind, and a veranda tacked across the front.

There were blankets in the big trunks in the front bedroom, packed away in mothballs and quite clean, only just dusted with the fine silvery sand that had seeped in everywhere. There were also four sleeping-bags.

'Save washing sheets,' Miles said practically.

When they started to put away the suitcases they found a Maori kit with them, filled with potatoes and kumaras; on top was a joint of pork wrapped in a white tea-towel.

'Mrs Lucy must have sent it with the men!' Callie said.

Miles asked: 'Can you cook pork?'

Mrs Mac thought pork too indigestible for children.

'I've never tried,' Callie admitted, 'but I don't

see why not. Once we get the stove going, that is.'

'Spiders!' Jo said, shuddering at the windows, which were crusted with cobwebs and salt spray.

'I'll do the windows,' Miles said grandly, 'I don't mind a few spiders.'

'I'll clean the floors then,' Jo said gratefully.

Callie attacked the stove, which was choked with soot and ashes, and Rory got down on his knees with the hearth broom, puffing like a train.

'One thing, this nice clean sand's not like dirt,' Jo said.

'*This* is like dirt,' Callie said grimly. Her hands were black.

She lighted a crumpled newspaper in the grate and billows of smoke rolled out, making everyone choke and cough. She wiped tears from her eyes.

'Perhaps there's something blocking the flu of the stove.'

'A bird's nest, perhaps,' Miles suggested. He climbed from the tank-stand to the roof, and presently Callie heard him give a shout of triumph.

She lighted another piece of paper and pulled out the damper, and there was a cheerful roar from the chimney.

'Now we can cook our pork!' Miles said in the doorway.

'I'm simply filthy!' Callie said.

'Let's swim!' Jo begged. 'We've done an awful lot of work.'

They put on their bathing-suits and rushed down over the sand. Rory came last, yelling crossly: 'Wait for me!' The sand was white and hot and silky under their feet, and the edge of the water so clear that it was like wading out into a magic mirror.

'Oh, it's beautiful, beautiful . . .' Callie said, sinking into the warm shallow water, but Rory splashed her and presently all four were leaping and screaming and splashing until they were quite worn out.

Finally Jo said: 'I'm *dying* of hunger!' and they rushed up to the house and cut themselves great hunks of bread and slices of cheese.

'This bread's not going to last,' Callie said, worried.

'Maybe we can learn to make bread,' Jo said with her mouth full. 'Or maybe we could get the bus to bring us some.'

'Mrs Lucy might know,' Miles suggested.

'We'll have to take her blankets back this afternoon,' Callie said.

'You and Jo go,' Miles said. 'I want to fish.'

He had found fishing-lines in the shed and a box of hooks.

'I want to go fishing too,' Rory announced firmly.

'Well, there you are then,' Miles said. 'It'll make it easier for you if you don't have him tagging after you all the way.'

They had sharp words because Miles wanted some pork for bait.

'It's *food*!' Callie cried. 'We're going to eat it! You can't go wasting it!'

'I'm not wasting it!' Miles shouted. 'I'm catching fish to eat!'

In the end they compromised. Callie cut off a small piece of the leanest part for Miles and a still smaller bit for Rory.

'You will look after him,' Callie begged suddenly. 'Don't let him fall off the rocks or anything!'

'Fuss, fuss, fuss!' said Miles. 'You're as bad as a grown-up. I'll tie a bit of line around his waist and then I can pull him back.'

Jo and Callie watched the two figures growing smaller as they trudged off down the beach, and then they went inside and put on clean shirts and shorts, and Callie brushed and plaited Jo's hair.

'It's only polite to make ourselves tidy.'

'What if we can't find our way?' Jo said fearfully. 'Or maybe we won't find anybody we know.'

'I don't see why we can't find our way,' Callie told her firmly; 'and if we don't know anyone, we'll just leave a message for Mrs Lucy.'

She sounded more confident than she felt. She wished Miles had come with them. She was not at all sure herself that she would know any of the dark-faced laughing men who had helped them the night before. She remembered only how kind everybody had been, and the comfort and warmth of the fire and meal after the rain and darkness outside.

It was easy to find their way across the tide channel and up the path. From the gap where the track narrowed they looked down on the surf that rolled on the rocks off the ocean side of the island. It was almost a sheer drop to the shore below, and Jo turned a little giddy and clung to the tussocks on the inner side.

'I remember this bit now. I always used to walk behind Father.'

In a moment the path widened again and they pushed on up through the wind-flattened scrub to the top of the ridge. Below them the brilliant blue sea spread away like a great sheet of silk to the far horizon; beyond each headland was another, fading out in the jewelled sea haze to the north.

'Isn't it marvellous?' Jo cried, tripping over a root in the track. 'It makes me feel I simply must go there!'

'Maybe we could,' Callie suggested recklessly. 'What's to stop us? We could take some food and sleeping-bags and camp out.'

They began to run over the far side of the ridge, downhill through the scrub. Soon they could see the blue tidal river and the little Maori settlement below them. Jo took a sudden fit of shyness.

'We don't even know which house it is!' she wailed.

'We can ask!' said Callie crossly, not too confident herself.

It all looked very comfortable and homelike, she thought, brown earth and green gardens and small, low houses following the loop of the sandy river. There were horses grazing on grassy patches and long rows of coloured washing hanging in the sun. In a big fenced garden women were working. One stood up and waved at the girls. It was Mrs Lucy.

'There you are, you see!' Callie said to Jo.

They climbed through the fence and crossed the furrows. The women were weeding kumara plants. Mrs Lucy crouched with her long skirts tucked under her. She had a black silk handkerchief tied over her hair.

'Where you fellows going?' she asked them.

'We came to return the blankets you lent us,' Callie said shyly, 'and to thank you very much for the pork and vegetables.'

'That's all right,' Mrs Lucy said easily. 'You want meat any time you can get the bus to leave it. Bread too. You can ring up from here.'

'Oh, thank you . . .' Callie said, much relieved.

'What you going to do for milk?' Mrs Lucy said suddenly.

Callie looked at her blankly. For some reason she had

never thought of milk; milk was something that was left at your gate in bottles. Miles and Jo and she could do without milk for a few weeks, but Rory would certainly need milk. She had a horrible vision of Rory wasting away, growing pale and thin with arms and legs like a Corso child, and all because she had been silly enough to forget that small boys needed milk.

'You better take a cow,' Mrs Lucy said.

Callie's mouth dropped open and she looked at Jo.

'I beg your pardon?' she said.

'Plenty cows knocking around here,' Mrs Lucy said off-handedly. 'They don't bother to milk them half the time. You take one home.'

It sounded as if a cow was something you put in your handbag.

'Oh . . .' Callie said, stammering, 'it's awfully kind of you, thank you very much, but I don't think we could keep it, we've no fences.'

Mrs Lucy looked at her in a pitying kind of a way.

'You can milk on shares with the calf,' she said.

'Oh . . . ?' said Callie blankly.

'Tie the calf up, put a *potae* on, can't drink, and the cow won't go away,' Mrs Lucy explained patiently as to a half-witted child. The girls looked so puzzled that everyone laughed long and loudly.

'Come and look!' said Mrs Lucy, and gathered her skirts and scrambled up as briskly as a girl. She led the girls through a gap in the hedge and showed them a black calf, stretched on his side in the shade, asleep. He wore a little woven flax basket, like a muzzle, over his nose and fastened with a loop of braided flax behind his ears.

'That's a *potae*,' she said, 'what you call a hat. He can't suck and his mother won't go very far away. At night you milk the cow and take off the *potae* and let the calf have a go, in the morning you put him on.'

'It's a wonderful idea!' Jo and Callie said together.

'Of course pakehas don't do it,' Mrs Lucy explained, 'because they want *all* the milk.'

She screamed suddenly at the top of her voice.

'Manuel! You go and get Rosie!'

'Rosie is a very quiet cow,' she told the girls.

There was no sign of Manuel, which annoyed Mrs Lucy very much, so she called a small girl and sent her off.

'That's Rosina. Luke's little girl.'

Callie found the relationships of Mrs Lucy's large family very confusing. Luke, she found, was the big handsome man working on the red truck near the house; he was the son of Mrs Lucy's last marriage. Paul and Manuel were the grandsons of the first marriage. The pretty girl, Rita, was Luke's wife, and the baby, Hadley, Mrs Lucy's youngest grandchild. It was all very puzzling, and the girls were struggling to get the relationships fixed in their mind when Rosina appeared again.

'Manuel's got the cow,' she announced.

Chapter 6

'I had all that I was now capable of enjoying.'
from *Robinson Crusoe*, by Daniel Defoe

For some reason Callie liked the sound of the name Rosie; she at once imagined a sweet little dark-eyed Jersey cow, but Rosie turned out to be red and angry-looking, as big as a horse, with a three-foot spread of wicked pointed horns. She rolled her eyes and shoved her calf crossly.

The calf was lovely, quite small and pure white, with a yellow patch on one eye and a few yellow freckles scattered around his pink muzzle.

'There you are,' said Mrs Lucy. 'I told you she was very quiet. You just pull the calf along and she'll go too.'

'Thank you very much,' said Callie in a trembling voice.

Rosie looked at the girls and made a groaning noise, and Callie stood and looked back at her, quite dismayed. It was left to Jo, who was afraid of nothing on four legs, to take charge, which she did happily.

'Isn't she *sweet*?' she said, patting Rosie's muscular red neck. 'Come on, Rosie, you're going to live with us now.

You push her, Callie, and I'll lead the calf on ahead.'

Mrs Lucy had sent somebody for a *potae*; she showed the girls how to fix the braided flax muzzle; they thanked her once again and then Jo led the white calf down the dusty road beside the river.

'You, Manuel,' Mrs Lucy ordered, 'go help them drive the cow.'

They travelled in a little procession, first Jo with the calf's lead rope, then Rosie, then Callie. Manuel trailed sulkily out of sight. They struck trouble when they started to climb the ridge. The calf stopped.

'Hasn't he got sweet little spots?' Jo said admiringly. 'What shall I do to make him go?'

'Hit him with a little bit of fern,' Callie advised.

Joe was pulling a stalk of fern when Freckles moved. He plunged downhill, ripping the rope from Jo's fingers, and next instant, head and tail high, he was tearing back down the hill. Rosie, bellowing loudly, galloped after, and the two girls panted in the rear. Callie had a wild moment of picturing the whole party arriving back at the pa.

However, Manuel came to the rescue. He pounced out of the scrub and threw himself on the trailing rope, and in a few seconds the girls came puffing up and the prancing calf and bellowing cow were once more turned in the direction of Penguin Island. Everyone had laughed so much that Manuel could no longer pretend to be shy; he pushed the calf and Jo pulled, and when they came to the narrow place in the track Callie was very glad to have his help in coaxing the stubborn Rosie.

'Under the willow tree at the back would be the nicest place to tie the calf,' Jo suggested, 'then Rosie can come and go as she likes.'

Miles and Rory came tearing up from the beach to see what was going on. Rory stood and stared at the little white calf, and then he stretched out a hand and touched the rough curly coat.

'I like it,' he announced. 'I'm going to call it Snowy.'

'You can't!' Jo shouted. 'It's not yours! It's called Freckles!'

'It's mine just as much as yours!' Rory screamed.

'You've got your old kitten!' Jo yelled. 'You want everything!'

'For goodness' sake,' said Callie, feeling like a grown-up, 'it belongs to everyone, so be quiet and stop quarrelling.'

Miles and Manuel were eyeing each other rather like two strange dogs.

After a moment Manuel muttered: 'You catch anything?'

'No,' Miles admitted, ashamed.

'You want to try pipi,' Manuel told him, 'for bait, I mean.'

The children looked blank. They knew that pipis were shellfish, but that was all. Manuel's face was pitying.

'I'll show you,' he said. 'You got a bag or something?'

The tide was low and they followed him out onto the flats and across the first channel towards a sandbank. He trod around, his toes curling and squirming, and then suddenly he pounced down and began scooping in the wet sand and brought up a triangular double shell. In a few moments he had tossed half a dozen into the bag which Callie carried.

'You got to be very quick. Else they dig down and you lost them.'

It seemed a lot easier than fishing, and the children all got very excited about it. In a few minutes they were all very wet and a great deal of sand was tossed everywhere. Even Rory dug like a little terrier.

'I can't find a single thing,' Jo wailed.

There was a loud scream from Rory. He was kneeling in the shallow water, soaking wet, his face scarlet.

'I got one! I got one!' he shouted.

He was clutching a large pipi in both hands, and even his hair stood up on his head with excitement. The bag was full before the children stopped digging and Miles had to help carry it.

'How do you cook them?' Callie asked Manuel.

'You're not going to cook them!' Miles shouted. 'They're for bait! You want to cook everything that comes into the house!'

'Of course I do!' Callie said crossly. 'We've got to eat.'

'You put them in fresh water,' Manuel told her. 'Get the sand out.'

Talking of cooking reminded Callie of the pork. She went into the house and started a fire in the stove. She was peeling potatoes when the others came in, and the fire was roaring merrily.

'Listen, all of you,' she said, 'I want some more wood. If I'm to do the cooking, someone else must get the wood. It's only fair.'

'I guess that's right,' Miles said, thinking it over. 'We have to organize things. Robinson Crusoe did. I'll get wood, and catch the fish.'

'I'll milk the cow,' Jo said eagerly, 'and I'll look after the calf.'

'I'll catch fish too,' Rory announced, 'and get wood with Miles.'

'You can get the kindling wood,' Callie told him. We'll need kindling every morning to start the fire.'

She put the potatoes and kumara in the pan with the pork and went out to see how Jo was getting on. They had put on the calf's *potae* when they tied him up, and now Jo had made up her mind to get a few drops of milk for tea. With a jug in one hand she was kneeling beside Rosie, tugging away patiently with the other hand at one of the long leathery teats.

'It seems much harder to get any milk from her than that cow I used to milk at Wairakei,' Jo panted, crawling along after Rosie as she moved.

'For goodness' sake don't get kicked!' Callie begged.

'Oh, I'm sure she wouldn't kick me,' Jo said, quite out of breath. 'It's just she's so tough . . . like an old boot or something . . .'

Ten minutes later she rushed into the house, her small jug half full.

'Look! Now we can have milk in our tea. Look, Callie! Look, Miles! Shall I make a cup of tea, Callie, so I can put some milk in it?'

Dinner was late. They made a driftwood fire in the living-room fireplace and sat around it, their plates on their knees. The pork was a little burned and the potatoes hard, but nobody complained. By the time they finished the meal darkness had come down outside, and they sat on sleepily in the light from the dying fire, hearing no sound but the faint swish of the ripples on the beach outside.

Suddenly there was a long-drawn, quavering cry.

The children sat still and looked at one another. Callie thought that she could feel the hair rising on the back of her neck, and Jo's eyes were as round as saucers.

'What is it?' Jo said in a shaking voice. 'It sounds like a baby . . .'

'Penguins,' Miles said unconvincingly.

There was another long, thin, pitiful cry, and Rory buried his face on Callie's knees.

'I don't like it,' he said gruffly, 'take it away.'

'It's Manuel's ghost!' Jo cried in a hysterical whisper. 'It lives up the river, and one time it followed his uncle all the way home ... and it *cried like a baby*!'

In another few seconds they would all have been hysterical. It was Miles who saved them. He grabbed up the poker from the fireplace.

'Don't talk such a lot of rot!' he said, his voice shaking. 'I'm going to open the door and see what's there ...'

'Oh no!' Jo cried, her voice shaking. 'Oh no, please don't open the door. *It* will come inside ...'

Miles looked at Callie and she nodded reluctantly.

'I suppose we must ...'

She pushed Rory off her knees and lighted a candle at the dying fire. With the candle in one hand and a stout stick of driftwood in the other, she joined Miles at the door. For a moment they looked at each other.

'Please don't open the door!' Jo begged, clasping Rory. 'I know something dreadful will come inside if you do ...'

Miles turned the handle slowly, and Callie held up the candle. In the gap of the opening door something moved, something dark which frightened Callie almost more than she had ever been frightened in her life before.

Next instant they were all rocking with laughter.

'It's a dog!' Rory cried, delighted.

It was a big black dog, long and lean, with one ear standing up, and one ear drooping. His face was furrowed with worried wrinkles. He stood in the doorway and put his head on one side and whined again. He had exactly the expression, Callie thought, of a man who turns up late and is not at all sure if there is room for him to spend the night.

'Isn't he beautiful?' Jo cried.

At the tone of her voice the dog walked forward into the room, sat down on the rug before the fireplace and beat his tail twice.

'Now we have a dog,' said Rory in a satisfied voice.

'A dog, a cat and a cow and a calf,' Jo said happily. 'We're much luckier than Robinson Crusoe, really, with his old parrot . . .'

'I'm going to name him!' Miles announced.

Callie shouted them all down.

'You don't know that we can keep this dog. He must belong to somebody. Maybe he's just visiting us . . .'

'He hasn't got a collar . . .' Miles said quickly.

'He thinks he belongs to us!' Jo cried, looking tearful.

The dog was now lying before the hearth. He thumped his tail.

'Anyway,' Callie said, 'dogs eat meat. How can we feed him?'

The others shouted her down.

'I'll catch fish for him!' Miles said.

'He can have my share of meat if you're going to be so mean!' Jo shrieked.

'He can eat pipis,' Rory said firmly.

'Anyway,' Jo said, much upset, 'I'm sure he's hungry now. Surely you'll let me give him a little piece of bread.'

The dog ate two slices of bread in two gulps, and then pushed the tin plate round and round the floor, clattering it. Callie sighed and cut him a piece of pork, which was there one minute and gone the next.

'I shall call him Percy,' Miles announced.

'Oh no,' Jo protested, 'that's not at all a nice name for a dog.'

'He eats just like that boy Percy who used to live next door,' Miles explained simply.

'Aren't we lucky?' said Jo contentedly. 'Now we have a dog we've got just everything we want.'

Chapter 7

'My island was now peopled, and I thought myself very rich in subjects.'

from *Robinson Crusoe*, by Daniel Defoe

It was the afternoon before Christmas when Callie suddenly began to feel thoroughly ashamed of herself. Not one of them, she realized, had spared a thought for poor Great-aunt Irene in hospital. They seemed to have been living in a little enchanted world of their own. She felt they could do nothing about Great-aunt Irene, but at least they could write to their father, who would be expecting a letter from them.

'I don't see how we can,' Miles objected. 'What about the postmark?'

'There must be some way of working it out,' Callie said slowly. 'Suppose we wrote a letter, put it in another envelope and sent it to the Auckland post office with some money, and a note saying we don't know what stamps to put on. Then it'd have the Auckland postmark.'

'I can't see what's wrong with that,' Miles agreed thoughtfully.

'Then we'll do it right away,' Callie said firmly.

'Dear Father,' she began on a sheet torn from an exercise book. 'We are all very well, and hope that you are well too, and not too cold.'

'Say something about the bus trip,' Miles suggested. 'You don't need to say which way the bus was going.'

'The bus trip was very interesting,' Callie wrote. 'It seemed a long way, but we had something to eat at lunch time . . .'

'Tell him we miss him,' Jo begged.

'Tell him about my kitten,' said Rory.

'Rory has a kitten, he calls it Toby, but I think it is a lady kitten. It is black and very playful, and follows him everywhere. We all miss you very much. Happy Christmas and love from us all, Callie.'

Even when Callie had finished the letter a feeling of depression dimmed her spirits. It seemed very queer to think of Christmas on their own, away from her father and all the family fun that had always meant Christmas to her. She wondered if the others felt the same: Jo looked a little forlorn, sitting on the steps, and Miles was idly gazing out to sea.

'Where are we going to find our tree?' she said in a determinedly cheerful voice.

'Our tree?' Jo said, springing up. 'Are we going to have a tree?'

'There's some little pines up the beach,' Miles put in.

'Of course we'll have a tree,' Callie said. 'We always have a tree for Christmas.'

In a cheerful bustle Miles ran to get the hatchet from the shed, and a length of rope, and they called Rory and set out. They found the little clump of seedling pines, but a great argument followed, as Miles wanted a tree which appeared to the girls to be quite twice as tall as the house itself. In the end they agreed upon a smaller one and took turns patiently chopping away with the blunt hatchet, and returned triumphantly along the beach, dragging their tree trunk first, harnessed to the rope like a team of ponies.

They planted the tree upright in a box of earth in the corner of the living-room, but decorations were a problem. The only coloured paper in the house was the silver wrapper from a bar of chocolate, and with that Jo covered a star for the top branch. Then Callie had a brain-wave.

'It'll be a *seaside* Christmas tree!' she announced. 'We'll hang it with strings of seaweed, and tie on our prettiest shells and those sea-egg cases we found, and put sand and shells over the earth in the box. And we can wrap the old fishing-net round the box . . . it'll look lovely!'

The tree did indeed look attractive, and Callie carefully unpacked the big parcel her father had given her to keep hidden. Inside were four smaller packages, wrapped in Christmas paper and labelled; Callie put them at the foot of the tree. The children were all a little worried that they had no presents to give one another; Mrs Mac had promised to take them shopping in Auckland. In the end Callie managed a necklace which she had scarcely worn to give Jo, a comb for Miles, and for Rory a jigsaw puzzle which she had been keeping for a wet day.

They planned to have lamb for dinner; Callie had got the butcher to send it up by bus. Mrs Lucy had sent kumaras and a kit of peaches. For the pudding the girls had experimented with a rather gluey mixture of flour and sugar and raisins all stirred up together, and tied in a cloth and boiled. Callie felt very doubtful about the result.

She was wakened very early on Christmas morning by Rory and the kitten dancing on her bed. 'Let's have the presents!' Rory was demanding. 'I've got a present for you!'

He had to wait while Miles dressed himself in Callie's red dressing-gown and tied a white handkerchief over his face to serve as a beard. Their father had always dressed up as Santa Claus to hand round the presents from the tree. All four of the parcels contained waterproof jackets, as light and soft as possible; the girls had silver charm bracelets too, and the boys had wonderful and complicated pocket-knives.

'Now you know why I had so little room in my suitcase!' Callie said, parading happily in her jacket. Rory had given her a boy's handkerchief, which he had never used, and she tucked it into her pocket.

'It's a lovely Christmas . . .' Jo said, sighing with pleasure. 'You'd think Father had known . . . let's go and swim now.'

They hurried into their bathing-suits. The weather was suddenly very warm; there was a pale blue haze over the hills and the water was glassy. Percy headed the procession down to the sea, and in a few seconds the children were all in the sea, which was clear and silky, almost as warm as the sunlight. The pattern of tiny shells and pebbles at the bottom was as bright as a carpet.

'I'm going to improve my swimming,' Jo said, and turned over and began to swim overarm. Miles was turning somersaults in the water, and Rory stood waist deep, lost in some game of his own. Percy pattered at the edge for a while, his face creased with worry, and then suddenly rushed in and knocked Rory down.

Callie was still laughing when she heard Jo's scream,

high and thin, cutting through the lazy-morning quiet. Jo was in deeper water than the others, and close beside her, out of the still water, Callie saw rise the curved and glistening flank of a huge fish.

It was a dreadful moment and it seemed to go on for ever. Callie saw Miles's face, like a mask of fright; she saw Rory, having picked himself up, standing and staring; nobody seemed able to move.

Then Miles was shouting and beating the water with his hands. Jo came splashing madly towards them and Callie was screaming back at Rory in the shallows: 'Get out of the water! Run, quick! It's a shark!'

Miles and Callie grabbed at Jo, and the three of them stumbled out after Rory. Callie was quite certain that the shark's snapping jaws were just behind them. She would never have believed how hard it was to hurry through waist-deep water. It seemed hours until they had splashed out onto the sand and into safety.

Jo was so weak with fright that they nearly had to carry her up the beach. She was shivering. Callie dropped down on the hot sand, her heart thumping madly. Rory's eyes were brimming with tears and Percy licked his toes to comfort him. Gradually they all began to feel a little better.

'Our beautiful beach!' Jo burst out with a wail. 'And on Christmas morning too! We'll never be able to swim here again!'

'Look!' said Miles tensely.

They stared at the bright water until their eyes burned.

Suddenly the surface broke and a dark curve slid into sight. In a moment, gracefully, the big fish rose up in a playful curve and vanished without a splash.

'It didn't look like a shark,' Miles breathed. 'Not like any picture I've ever seen. And its head was different somehow.'

'I thought you were supposed to see a shark's fin,' Callie whispered. They were all whispering. 'And do sharks *jump*?'

At that moment the fish jumped again. Before the children's unbelieving eyes it arched upwards, somersaulted and was gone.

It was Callie who realized it first.

'It's a dolphin!' she shrieked.

For a moment they were quite bewildered by the discovery, and then they jumped to their feet and ran back to the water's edge.

'That book I was reading . . .' Callie murmured; 'their heads are that funny shape . . . not snouty like a shark's. And in the pictures they were jumping just like that. And they *like people*, they come close to shore and follow swimmers and boats . . .'

They were getting over their fright and they ventured into the water again, standing waist deep, looking out to sea.

'How I wish he would come back . . .' Jo said.

'The Greeks taught them to come to a bell,' said Callie. 'There was a story about a boy on an island, and he had a tame dolphin that used to swim into the cove when he rang his little bell . . .'

Callie stopped talking. Behind her the dolphin was moving through the water. He was so close that she could see his small twinkling eyes, set among deep wrinkles, the long rippling curve of his glistening flank.

They stood silent, watching, and, having passed so close to them, he turned and swam straight out to sea. In a minute they saw him break the still water out in the bay.

'I'm hungry,' Rory said.

'I suppose we must go and put the Christmas dinner on,'

Callie said dreamily. They walked up the beach, all un-
usually silent, the warmth of the sun and the sparkle of
the water around them.

'I shall give him a name,' Callie said. 'Everybody has
something else, and I am going to name the dolphin.'

'Wasn't he the loveliest Christmas present?' Jo sighed.

'I shall call him Gabriel,' Callie told them.

'Is it reverent?' Jo asked doubtfully. 'Gabriel was an
angel.'

'There is', said Callie, 'nothing irreverent about a
dolphin.'

Chapter 8

'We had fished for some time and catcht nothing.'
from *Robinson Crusoe*, by Daniel Defoe

The afternoon of Christmas Day was very hot. The children dragged a mattress out under the shade of the willow tree. Callie had a book, and Jo hung over her shoulder, enchanted by the illustrations.

'Oh, it's all about sea-birds . . . now we'll be able to find out all the names. See, those dear little grey birds that run along the sand like chickens . . . dotterels. Where did you get it?'

'It was on the top shelf,' Callie said. 'It's got Father's name in it. Look: "For John Eliot, from the author, Francis Gilroy".'

'Professor Gilroy,' Jo said thoughtfully. 'Didn't he once come to see us at Wairakei? An old man with a grey moustache?'

'And he showed us slides of all sorts of birds and their nests.'

'He was nice,' Jo said, 'I liked him. Oh, look at the

picture of the oyster-catchers. Aren't they lovely?'

Rory was already asleep, with Toby draped across his bare legs. Soon Callie was the last person awake. It was very hot. Percy panted in his sleep and his long pink tongue lolled out. At last Callie slept, and she dreamed that she was riding round the bay on a tame dolphin whose coat gleamed like gold in the sunshine.

They all woke hungry and thirsty, and Callie put the kettle on.

'I don't know why we need to eat so much,' she sighed.

'I'll get some pipis for tea,' Miles suggested. Callie thought he was getting a little tired of promising them fish. She had not been at all successful in cooking pipis; because they had seemed so tough she had boiled them for half an hour, and they had tasted like small pieces of boot leather rolled in salt and sand. Only Percy would eat them.

'I guess we'll try fishing instead,' Callie said firmly.

When it was cooler they took their lines and climbed the hill, and followed the faint track which led down the ocean side through groves of flax bushes and wind-twisted karaka trees hung with yellow berries. Great boulders and slabs of rock lined the shore. They found a comfortable ledge, close to deep water, and baited their lines and threw them out. Callie sat close to Rory so that she could grab him. It was very pleasant sitting there watching the sea, but nothing seemed to be happening.

Jo sighed.

'Maybe there aren't any fish around. People are always saying that fishing's not like it used to be.'

There was a peculiar little noise from Rory. He was staring at his line, which was stretched taut.

'Something is there . . .' he said in a hoarse voice.

61

They all rushed at him, and Miles grabbed the line just as Rory was about to overbalance after it. It jerked through his hands.

'It's heavy . . .' he gasped. 'It must be a fish . . .'

'Be careful, be careful!' Jo beseeched.

'Slowly!' Callie cried at him. 'Not so fast . . . pull slowly . . .'

His eyes wild and his hair on end, Miles drew in the line, and in a few seconds a big beautiful silvery fish broke clear of the water, leaping and struggling. It fell into a cleft in the rocks at the water's edge, and Rory broke into bellowing yells of misery.

'It's gone! You've lost it!'

Miles thrust the wet tangle of line into his hands and leaped down and grabbed the wriggling fish. It slipped from his grasp, but he scooped it up again and threw it farther up the rocks to safety. While Jo looked the other way, he produced his new knife and neatly slit the fish and cleaned it as he remembered his father doing. The children stood round and marvelled at their catch.

'Isn't it beautiful?' Jo breathed. 'Look at the silvery colours.'

'It's so *big*,' Callie said thankfully. 'Two meals at least.'

Only Rory said nothing at all. Excitement had left him white and silent, but after a little time he began to boast unbearably.

'I caught a fish. Nobody else has caught a fish. Not Callie, not Jo, not Miles. Miles is cross because he hasn't caught a fish yet . . .'

'Oh, you horrid little boy!' Callie said reprovingly.

At that moment Jo began to shriek and leap about. She had a fish on her line and Miles rushed to help her. It was a small snapper, and Jo was so thrilled with it that Callie was afraid she was going to insist upon putting it back in the water again, but Miles wasted no time in killing it.

It was all very exciting. Before another few minutes had gone by Callie landed another kahawai, smaller than Rory's, and then Jo hooked something big which got off her line. Still Miles had caught nothing. After another half-hour they decided that the tide was past its best, and they rolled up their lines. Miles was looking very sober.

'Isn't it marvellous?' Jo said happily. 'We have so much fish that even Percy can have a really good feed.'

In a little while Callie saw that she was crying. Her large tears fell into the sand, and Percy leaped up and gazed unhappily into her face.

'What's the matter now?' Callie said resignedly.

'I can't bear to think that someone may come and take Percy away!'

Her tears fell so fast that she knelt down and buried her face in Percy's rough coat. The others all stood round and gazed very gloomily.

'I *told* you not to get too fond of him!' Callie said accusingly.

In a very few days they had all grown much too fond of Percy. It seemed as if he had been a member of their family for years.

'Nobody's going to take Percy away!' Rory shouted. In a minute he was going to be crying too.

'For heaven's sake!' said Callie, trying to be sensible. 'We'll go over tomorrow and see if Mrs Lucy knows anything about him. The longer we keep him the worse it'll be. And now let's go home and cook our fish.'

Miles cut pieces from the kahawai Rory had caught, and Callie rolled them in salt and oatmeal, and fried them in butter in the old black pan.

'This is my fish. I have eaten my fish,' Rory chanted sleepily.

The long day in the sunshine had been too much for him, and he fell asleep with his head in his plate. Callie had to carry him to bed.

She pulled back the faded curtain and leaned for a moment on the sill of the open window. Jo came and stood beside her. There was a gold moon hanging low over the water and everything smelled very sweetly of salt and sand and sea-grass. A bird flew overhead crying sadly.

'It's been the most marvellous Christmas Day . . .' Jo murmured.

'I wonder where Gabriel is,' Callie said.

For breakfast next morning they had more fish and sliced potatoes. Callie looked ruefully into the empty cupboard—no flour, butter, porridge or sugar, and the tea was nearly finished.

'We'll go over right away to Mrs Lucy's and ring up for an order to be sent on the bus. Now think, everybody, what do we want?'

'Bones for Percy,' Jo suggested.

It was a pity that she had thought of Percy. The others tried not to look at her. There was some argument about who should go over to Mrs Lucy's, but Miles wanted to dig pipis for bait, and Rory decided to stay with him. Jo was terrified that they would find Percy's owner, yet she would not let him go without her for fear she would never see him again.

In the end she went with Callie, and they took the snapper she had caught as a present for Mrs Lucy. Percy was the only one who seemed to enjoy the walk over the hill; he ranged back and forth and barked without a care in the world at the seagulls that flew overhead.

The first person they met was Manuel with two small boys and a yellow dog. The yellow dog and Percy bristled at each other.

'I see you got Ned Barry's dog,' Manuel observed.

Jo went scarlet and quite forgot to be shy.

'What do you mean, Ned Barry's dog? This isn't anybody's dog, he's a stray dog, he came to us because he was just about starving!'

'Ned's dog all right,' Manuel returned calmly. 'He had it when he was a pup.'

Jo would not let Callie get a word in.

'Well, where is this Ned Barry now?' she demanded.

'Gone to Australia, I guess,' asid Manuel. 'That's where he started to go, him and his missus and the kids.'

'You mean they just went and left this poor dog?' Jo screamed.

'Oh no,' Manuel explained, 'they gave him to Rangi Mitchell up the river to hunt pigs, but he wouldn't stop there, I guess no kids or something, he was always a great one for going around with the kids. Anyway, Rangi's got three dogs already. I guess he doesn't want any more.'

'You mean', said Jo and Callie together, quite slowly, 'that nobody really wants this dog?'

'I guess so,' said Manuel cheerfully.

Immediately Jo's tears overflowed. She knelt down and cried into Percy's rough coat.

'What's the matter with her?' said Manuel, surprised.

'Oh, nothing,' Callie said. It was too complicated to explain.

When they found Mrs Lucy Jo rushed straight up to her.

'Oh, Mrs Lucy,' she gabbled, 'Manuel says nobody wants this dog, and is that true, and do you think it's all right for us to keep him?'

By the time Callie had explained the whole thing over again, Mrs Lucy understood what they were talking about. She shook her head briskly.

'Rangi doesn't want him, he said so. You keep him, he'll be a watchdog for you, it's not good for you to be by yourselves.'

'And don't you dare start crying again!' Callie said to Jo fiercely.

The journey that had seemed so long and anxious was almost too short as they retraced their steps, running most of the way, leaping from tussock to tussock, with Percy racing ahead. They tore barefooted up the beach and arrived at the little grey house quite out of breath.

'It's all right, we can keep him!' Jo screamed.

'Mrs Lucy says nobody wants him!' Callie panted.

'Ned Barry has gone to Australia and Rangi has three dogs already!'

'And Mrs Lucy gave us some yeast and told me how to make bread . . .'

'And she laughed and laughed at us boiling the pipis for an hour, she said it makes them tough, you just put them in boiling water . . .'

'We got heaps of pipis,' Miles said as he and Rory danced round the wildly excited Percy.

At last, quite exhausted by excitement, Percy sank down and laid his head on his paws and panted. Jo dropped down beside him.

'Darling, darling Percy . . .' she murmured. 'Now you shall live with us for ever.'

Chapter 9

'At length I spy'd a little cove.'
from *Robinson Crusoe*, by Daniel Defoe

That afternoon the children planned to make an expedition across the island and along the beach to the seaward end. Percy led the little procession and Toby brought up the rear.

'I don't know why you didn't shut her up,' Miles said resignedly. 'Now I suppose we shall have to carry her all the way home.'

Rory stamped indignantly.

'She shan't be shut up! She wants to come on the picnic just like us!'

It was very hot going down the far side of the hill. Their tracks led them through a little sheltered valley patched with bush and nikau palm trees, and smelling sweetly of sunburned grass. Near to the shore the palms gave way to groves of wind-blown karaka trees and old gnarled pohutukawas that overhung the tumbled rocks.

Callie stood and shaded her eyes and stared northwards.

'See that headland away up there, just about disappearing into the haze? It looks like a lion crouching . . .'

'Let's go up there some time,' Jo begged. 'You said we could. It would be such fun to walk and walk, and not have to come back at night.'

'I don't see why we shouldn't,' Miles allowed thoughtfully. 'We could carry our sleeping-bags and the billy and some food and our fishing-lines and matches. We wouldn't need much else . . .'

'We'd have to pick fine weather,' Callie said. 'We'd find plenty of sheltered places for sleeping out.'

'We could sleep in a cave,' Miles suggested, savouring the thought.

'Toby will come,' said Rory threateningly.

'Oh yes!' said Miles. 'And Rosie and the calf too, I suppose!'

'I wonder when Father will get our letter,' Jo said thoughtfully, 'and if he will think there is anything funny about it?'

'I don't see why he should,' Callie said in an uneasy voice. 'Of course it was a very short letter, wasn't it? And we didn't say anything about Aunt Irene, because we couldn't. Maybe he'll just think we're very bad letter-writers.'

'I expect so,' Jo said, cheering up. 'Oh, look, look! The little penguins, aren't they sweet?'

There was a little group of blue penguins ducking and diving in the wash of the sea beyond the rocks. The children sat and watched them, and then pushed on their way again. It was a rough scramble over the rocks, and presently they clambered farther up the hill again, clinging to the tussocks and wind-blown flax bushes.

Toby sat down and mewed and Jo picked her up and

A little blue penguin

carried her. A rough sort of half-track led them around a shoulder of the hill and down again toward the beach, where their way was barred by two tremendous rocks leaning toward one another and towering to the hill above. Between the two was a narrow cleft with a glimpse of the sea.

The children stood and eyed the barrier almost with awe. There was no way on but through the cleft.

'It's like the Rock of Ages in the hymn,' Jo said. 'You know, "Rock of Ages, cleft for me . . ."'

Miles went first, stooping, and sliding sideways through the opening. The others followed him, and then stood still, staring around them.

A rocky bay enclosed a crescent-shaped beach of pure white sand. A small stream flowed in pale blue curves from the hill to the sea, and over it the pohutukawa trees leaned protectingly. The final touch of perfection was a long sweep of delicate seashells, which lay as the tide had left them on the rippled sand.

Almost breathlessly the children descended to the untrodden beach.

'Oh look!' Jo cried. 'Look at the shells! Aren't they the most beautiful things you ever saw?'

Then she gave a scream. 'Oh, look! What is it?'

The four of them gathered wonderingly around the thing that lay at the far end of the curve of shells, a great transparent bubble like a witch's crystal.

'It's magic,' said Rory, touching it with an awed finger.

'I think it's a glass float,' Callie said as softly. 'You know, the kind the fishing boats use for their nets. It's probably come from a Japanese boat, I should think . . .'

'It must be one of those places where things come up,' Rory said with shining eyes. 'Look, here's a piece of rope. Now we have a real shipwrecked sailor's beach . . .'

It was very hot and they threw themselves down on the dry, white sand in the shade. The red fallen blossom from the pohutukawa trees lay on the rocks around them. Jo and Rory played with the shells, and Callie gathered small pieces of driftwood, while Miles cut two stakes and a cross-piece to boil the billy. They filled it where the stream ran down out of the hill.

Callie cut up Mrs Lucy's loaf with Miles's knife. They had no butter, but the bread was fresh and crusty and sweet, and the tea smelled of driftwood smoke. Toby slept stretched out on a rock, and Percy sat on his haunches, looking from one to the other, hoping that a piece of bread would be left for him.

'I wonder why more people don't do this,' Jo said.

'Grown-ups, I mean, people with money. I can't think of anything they could do with money that would be as much fun as this.'

'I like this place,' Rory stated.

'Well, you're to stop here in the shade for a while,' Callie told him. 'We all will. Then we'll have a swim, and go home when it's a bit cooler.'

In ten minutes Rory was asleep, Percy panting heavily beside him. Jo played with her shells, and Callie lay gazing drowsily into the Chinese puzzle of the pohutukawa branches above her. A pair of tuis flew from limb to limb, their wings rustling stiffly, like old-fashioned silk. They sang in liquid notes like flute music, and quarrelled harshly, and made it up, and sang again.

It was still hot when the children stirred themselves and went down to swim. The water was cool and smooth, and Callie closed her eyes and floated, her wet hair drifting about her face. Some movement in the water startled her, and she stood up, waist deep, and looked about her.

The water swirled, and not three feet from her, so close that she could almost have touched him, a bottle-nosed face, wrinkled and bright-eyed, looked into hers, and a long, curved, shining flank passed her by.

'It's Gabriel!' Jo cried in a scream of delight.

Three times Gabriel passed between them, quite slowly, playfully, and then he headed out toward the sea, gave a rollicking bound, and was gone.

'Isn't he *wonderful*?' Jo said, with tears in her eyes. 'Oh, I do love Gabriel!'

'Don't any of you,' said Callie quite fiercely, 'any time, tell anybody about him!'

'Whom could we tell?' Miles asked reasonably.

71

They took one last look at the little bay

'Manuel,' said Callie, 'or even Mrs Lucy. And people might come, and frighten him or something.'

'Oh, they know,' Miles said. 'Manuel told me about him. He often comes, they say, when the kids go out to the mouth of the river to swim. They don't take any notice of him.'

'Well, so long as no outside people ever get to know . . .' Callie said with a pang of uneasiness.

The appearance of the dolphin had set the final seal of pleasure on the day. The children dried themselves in the sunshine and prepared to start home. Rory was given the empty billy, tied by a piece of flax across his shoulders,

Jo carried Toby and Callie the glass fishing float. Miles was laden down by his piece of rope, two short lengths of wave-worn timber and a broken crayfish pot which he had found.

'It's going to seem a long way home to you,' Callie warned him.

'I can take my time,' Miles said. 'If I get tired I'll leave the timber half way, and get it another day.'

It took him some trouble to get his burdens through the cleft in the rocks, and then they all took one last look at the little bay, calm and peaceful in the late afternoon sunlight.

'We should give it a name,' Jo said lovingly. 'What shall we call it?'

'Gabriel's Bay,' said Callie.

Chapter 10

'It cost me much labour.'
from *Robinson Crusoe*, by Daniel Defoe

It was a great pity, Callie thought afterwards, that Miles ever found the crayfish pot. It led to a lot of trouble.

He had to make a second trip next day to fetch home his salvaged timber, and, when Jo asked him what he intended to do with it, he was a little short-tempered and told her not to ask silly questions. Good timber, he said, always came in handy sooner or later.

However, he fell to work immediately upon the crayfish trap, patching the hole with carefully twisted wire.

'I'm going to set it out in the rocks,' he informed the girls. 'Manuel will know a good place. Then we'll have crayfish for dinner. Boy, this is certainly a good place, where you can get things like crayfish out of the sea for nothing! The way we're going with fish and all, we soon won't have to buy anything at all!'

'Except things like bread and butter and tea and sugar,'

said Callie dampeningly. 'We can't catch *them* in a crayfish pot.'

'I thought you were going to make bread,' Miles countered, 'and if Jo didn't give the calf so much milk we might even be able to make our own butter.'

'I don't see why the crayfish don't just turn right round and walk out again,' Jo said, examining the trap.

'Because they're too silly,' Miles explained. 'The place where they come in is wider on the outside . . . see? . . . and they push their way in to get at the bait, and when they turn round again they don't know how to push the wires apart to get out again.'

'They must be very silly,' said Rory flatly.

'They're very good to eat though, aren't they?' Jo said. 'I mean, people in books are always having dinner parties with lobster and champagne and things like that. Oh, let's have a dinner party, Callie, when we get our crayfish, it would be such fun!'

'What about the champagne?' Miles asked.

'Oh, lemon drink would do,' Jo said. 'Mrs Lucy would give us some lemons. And there must be recipes in that big recipe book in the cupboard . . .

She rushed inside at full speed and rushed out again, carrying the book under her arm, and sat down cross-legged on the sand.

'Here we are . . . this sounds lovely . . . "Lobster Newburg" . . . crayfish is like a lobster, isn't it? "Two tablespoons of butter, a glass of dry sherry, a pinch of cayenne, fresh cream . . ."'

Her voice trailed off a little, and after a minute she shut the book firmly.

'I expect it would be very nice just boiled.'

Miles had finished with the trap; he was going over the

75

hill, he said, to see Manuel and ask him what bait to use.

'Bring back some lemons!' Jo screamed after him. 'Mrs Lucy said we could have some whenever we wanted.'

'Let's have some nice pudding tonight,' she begged Callie. 'Something nice for our dinner party.'

'I don't know what makes you think Miles is going to catch something in that old trap,' Callie said pessimistically. 'I should think he could set it every day for months and never get a crayfish.'

'I just feel he's going to,' said Jo with hope in her voice. 'Let's get something nice ready, and have our dinner party, please, Callie!'

'Oh, all right,' Callie agreed. 'We can eat the pudding at least. What about an apple pie; are there any more apples on that tree down the beach?'

'Can you make apple pie?' Jo asked doubtfully.

'I don't see why not,' Callie said, thinking it over. 'So long as that stupid recipe book doesn't say all sorts of things we haven't got.'

The recipe book, however, asked for only flour and salt and butter, and Jo produced half a basket of wormy green apples, which she sat down to peel and core, while Callie stoked up the fire.

'We'll make it now,' she decided, 'and then we can have it cold.'

Their combined efforts turned out a quite respectable looking pie; Jo trimmed the edges, and Callie placed the dish reverently in the hot oven.

'Don't keep on opening the door to look!' she shouted at Jo after a few minutes. 'You're letting heat out!'

'But I'm so afraid it will burn!' Jo wailed.

'What's the nice smell?' Miles wanted to know, coming in. 'We've put out the trap in that rocky bit there, on the other side, near where the track comes down.'

Jo laid the table hopefully, having unearthed a white tablecloth from one of the cupboards, and washed and ironed it. The iron had to be heated on top of the stove, and left one or two black marks, but the whole effect was quite good. She put out two candles in candlesticks and filled a vase with stems of the fluffy-tailed sea-grass. There were four glasses that did not match, and she set one at each plate.

'There!' she breathed. 'Doesn't that look beautiful? Just like a *banquet*! How long will the crayfish take to cook?'

'Most people', said Callie, 'wait to catch one before worrying about cooking it.'

But for once Callie was to be proved wrong. The pie was not long cooled, and Jo was just coming back from milking the cow, when triumphant shouts could be heard coming over the hill. The two girls rushed round to the back of the cottage and met Miles and Rory, jog-trotting down the path, carrying between them a long stick from which hung the crayfish trap. They were both scarlet in the face with excitement, and both panting loudly.

'There!' said Miles, as they dumped their burden on the ground. 'It's not everybody who can go out and catch a crayfish just like that!'

'It's not everybody who can catch a crayfish just like that!' Rory echoed faithfully.

The crayfish was medium-sized, dark green and malignant-looking, with waving claws and wicked protruding eyes.

Jo fell back with a faint wail.

'I thought it would be dead . . .'

'Dead!' Miles cried indignantly as if she were somehow blaming him. 'Why should it be dead?'

'I don't know ...' Jo said, quite disorganized. 'Drowned ... maybe ...'

'Drowned!' said Miles. 'You're mad. Why should it drown when it lives in the water?'

'Then how do we kill it?' Callie asked.

Fascinated, they all stood around the trap and its fearsome captive. Miles seemed a little uncomfortable.

'Manuel says,' he began, 'Manuel says that you throw it into a pot of boiling water.'

Jo gave a piercing shriek of outraged horror, and even Callie turned a little pale.

'Oh no!' Jo wailed. 'Oh no, we couldn't do anything like that! Let it go again, Miles, quick! Put it back in the water!'

'Put it back in the water!' Miles yelled. 'After all our trouble! Are you mad?'

'Well, can you kill it?' Callie wanted to know.

Miles looked thoughtful. They all drew closer and regarded the crayfish carefully, and it appeared to turn its unpleasant, stalk-like eyes in their direction.

'It's really rather sweet,' Jo murmured, and Rory turned his angelic smile upward toward Callie.

'I shall call it Amy,' he announced.

Miles gave a yell of rage.

'Now look at that!' he demanded. 'Calling crayfish names, won't have them killed, won't have them eaten, next thing you'll be keeping them for pets! Whose idea was it, anyway, to have a big crayfish dinner?'

'But I didn't know you had to boil them alive,' Jo said, quite humbly. 'Please don't be cross, Miles. We could keep it in our aquarium on the beach when we get it fixed.'

78

'It would be an awful nuisance fixing it up to keep in anything like a crayfish,' Miles said grudgingly, but he appeared to be thinking the problem over.

'Let's go in,' said Callie, 'and eat the apple pie.'

In the morning Amy was still there, moving crossly around in the trap which Miles had anchored in shallow water. Jo gathered a tin full of small crabs from the sand-flats and offered them to her, but Amy merely swivelled her long-stalked eyes about and stared unblinkingly.

'I expect she's shy,' Jo explained.

'Come on,' Miles said briskly, hustling everybody. 'Let's get started on the aquarium or we'll never get it done.'

He had chosen a rock pool at the far end of the beach. They set off, dragging a spade, hammer and nails, stakes and a roll of rusty wire-netting that had been lying in the grass at the back of the cottage.

'How are you going to stop Amy eating everything else in the pool?' Callie wanted to know.

'Oh well, if you're going to make difficulties all the time . . .' Miles said crossly. He thought it over. 'We'll make it in two parts, one half a sort of pen for Amy and anything big, like eels, and the other just a pool for little fish and sea-anemones and so on. Let's get started, for goodness' sake.'

By lunch time the pen appeared secure enough to them to fetch Amy and release her from her trap. She immediately disappeared under a large rock and stayed there, only her feelers in sight.

'Well, she's not going to be very interesting if she stays there all the time,' Jo said, disappointed.

'Maybe she'll get used to coming out for food,' Callie said, more hopefully than she felt.

'Well, I'm hot,' Miles said. 'I'm going to swim.'

They were wearing their bathing-suits, which seemed to grow more shrunken and faded every day. They laid down their tools thankfully, and waded out into the rising tide.

'I wonder if Gabriel will come,' Jo said.

Miles was looking up at the sky.

'The weather looks funny,' he said. 'I think we must be going to have rain.'

It was very warm, but there was no sun. The sky was covered with a skim of thick curdled cloud. No wind moved and the sea looked like a sheet of dull glass.

'It seems funny,' Jo said, 'all the time we've been here it's been so fine and still. Somehow I can't imagine a storm here.'

'We'd better get wood after dinner,' Callie said a little anxiously. 'It would be awful if we had no dry wood.'

There was plenty of driftwood towards the far end of the beach. The children made two trips and dragged home as much as they could carry, and piled it in the shelter of the back porch, and Callie stacked the wood-box in the living-room with dry kindling wood. Jo milked Rosie early and let the calf go with her, and took some more crabs to Amy sulking under her rock.

After the long, lazy sunny days and golden evenings it was depressing to see the mist settle down over the sea, and grey afternoon turn to dusk. Callie lighted a fire in the living-room and set two precious candles on the table to make them feel more cheerful. Before they went to bed the rain began.

Chapter 11

'By this time it blew a terrible storm indeed.'
from *Robinson Crusoe*, by Daniel Defoe

Callie woke some time in the night to hear the wind screaming by. The little house seemed to cower in the sandhills as sheets of water were flung at it. Under all the noise of the wind and rain Callie could hear a low vibrating thunder, like the beating of drums. She sat up in bed and struck a match and found Rory standing in the doorway in lop-sided pyjamas, Toby clutched tightly in his arms.

'It's raining,' he offered.

'Yes, I know,' Callie agreed. She lighted the candle.

'It's not me that minds the storm,' Rory announced bravely. 'Toby doesn't like it.'

'Bring her and get into bed with me,' Callie suggested. 'Perhaps that'll cheer her up.'

Rory gave a sigh of relief and pattered across the room and climbed onto the bed, still clutching the unprotesting kitten. He settled down, comforted, as another fierce gust of wind shook the little house.

'What makes the other noise, Callie?' he wanted to know. 'All that sort of rumbling?'

'Why, it's only the sea,' Callie reassured him. 'It's the waves on the other side of the island. They can't hurt us, it's nice hearing them.'

Satisfied, Rory settled down, and soon Callie too was asleep. Some time in the early morning she awakened to find the house shaking under a terrific roll of thunder. Before she could get the candle alight, the blue glare of another flash of lightning turned everything to day, and a stunning crash of thunder broke overhead.

The candle, when she lighted it, was very small and feeble, and in its light Jo's head appeared above her blankets; she looked pale and round-eyed with fright. In the doorway was Miles, with Percy, who whimpered loudly.

'I don't *like* it!' Rory announced, hands over ears.

Callie got out of bed and struggled into her old dressing-gown. Her hands were shaky. She had always been nervous of thunderstorms.

'Come on, we'll light the fire,' she said, trying to sound quite calm and grown up. 'It'll make it more cheerful. Come on, Rory, bring Toby.'

She had taken three steps when a wicked double flash stabbed through the house. Rory clutched her silently, Percy howled, and a crash like the end of the world burst about their ears.

With trembling hands Callie began lighting all the candles she could find, and then fell on her knees and thrust crumpled paper and bits of kindling into the fire-place. She felt that a fire would be a comfort, but before it could blaze up, Miles pointed to the front door.

'Look . . .' he said.

From under the door a small gush of water was creeping.

'We're flooded!' Jo cried in a wail.

Callie hastily pulled aside the window curtain and another flash of lightning made her jump back.

'It's the sea,' she said. 'The wind's backing it up, I suppose, and it's a spring tide, and the waves are breaking right up the steps.'

'Will it wash us away?' Rory demanded.

'Of course not!' Callie reassured him. 'After all, this house has been here for years and years, before you were born, why should it get washed away now? The tide will turn soon, and the thunder is going away.'

'I don't want to go back to bed yet,' Jo said rather faintly.

'Well, we won't,' Callie agreed. 'We'll put on the kettle and have cocoa and make some toast. That'll cheer us all up.'

'Breakfast in the middle of the night!' Rory exclaimed, pleased.

They kept a wary eye on the door, but only an occasional spurt of water was finding its way in, and presently none at all. The rain continued, and the thunder rocked and rolled around the hills, but the peak of the storm seemed to be past. The children sat around the fire and ate hot toast thickly spread with butter, and brought out the old pack of cards and played Old Maid in the candlelight, and presently, when dawn began to show grey at the windows, they went back to bed.

They all slept half way through the morning, and when they got up the wind had slackened. Rain still fell, but the tide had ebbed.

'Let's put on our new jackets,' Callie suggested, 'and climb to the top of the hill and look at the sea.'

They struggled up the slippery track and at the top of the hill they stood entranced. The ocean was a wild grey-and-white plain. To the north the coast was wrapped in a haze of yeasty foam and spindrift. Below them the great white-maned swells came cascading in, flinging clouds of spray; the crests rose, curled over and hurled themselves on the rocks with a thunder that shook the island.

The scene was so exciting that the children began to run along the crest of the hill, to dance on the wet grass and scream as a monster roller struck the rocks and fountains of spray hurtled upward.

'Look!' Miles shouted, pointing. 'We couldn't get off now if we wanted to. We're really living on an island!'

The waves were driving over the crossing between the island and the mainland; the foamy crests swirled into the quieter waters of the bay. The sight sobered Callie a little. She took Rory's cold wet hand.

'Come on,' she said, 'we'll go home and get dry.'

They were very relieved to find Rosie sheltering comfortably, with Freckles, in a clump of giant flax bushes. Callie was cutting bread for lunch when Miles came in, looking very upset.

'All that work for nothing!' he scolded. 'All my aquarium is washed away. I can't even find the wire-netting!'

'Oh, whatever has happened to Amy?' Jo wailed.

'She's gone too,' Miles announced with gloomy satisfaction.

'Just as well,' said Callie heartlessly.

'I don't suppose she did have a very nice nature,' Jo mourned.

By mid afternoon the rain had stopped and a ragged patch of pale blue sky showed above the eastern horizon.

Pied shag, one of the many birds they saw on the shore

When the tide was well out Miles organized an expedition to their beachcombers' cove to see what the storm had brought.

The sea was less violent, but the children kept well above the beach and scrambled cautiously along the wet hillside. Carefully they stooped and slipped through the cleft in the rocks.

'Be careful of the waves!' Callie begged.

The beach was a wild jumble of sea-wrack, of tangled kelp and driftwood and heaped shells. The children scrambled amongst the tangle, searching and exploring. It was Miles who found the oar with the splintered haft. There was a name cut into it—*Sandpiper*.

'Do you suppose someone has been wrecked?' Jo begged, awestruck.

Rory had wandered a little way along the beach and now he rushed back, red in the face and important.

'I've found a box!' he announced.

'Perhaps it's treasure!' Jo panted.

It did not look at all like treasure. The box was a very ordinary wooden one, broken at one end. Miles took a stick of driftwood and forced up the broken boards.

'It's *food*!' he said.

There were several pounds of butter, rather badly knocked about, some tins with the labels washed off, and a strangely shaped object that turned out to be a large piece of bacon in a muslin bag.

'This is a wonderful place!' Miles exulted. 'We can even get food out of the sea! It's just like a proper desert island. Now we can have bacon and eggs for breakfast.'

'It looks a bit funny,' Callie said doubtfully.

'How are we going to carry it back?' Jo wanted to know.

'You girls always make difficulties,' Miles said crossly. 'And there's nothing the matter with the bacon. It's just been in the sea.'

'It looks funny to me,' Callie said stubbornly.

After a great deal of organizing upon Miles's part they set out for home. Callie carried the tins and Jo had the butter. Rory dragged the broken oar, while Miles toiled along under the weight of the bacon slung across his shoulders.

'I don't care,' he panted as they scrambled up the slippery hillside, 'there's not many people can just go out like us and pick up their food on the beach!'

Chapter 12

'It was my lot . . . to fall into pretty good company.'
from *Robinson Crusoe*, by Daniel Defoe

The morning after the storm was dazzlingly fine. The beach was littered with drifts of dirty foam and heaps of seaweed, but the seagulls were back in the water, floating silently in the tide channels and wheeling overhead. Percy chased them, scattering bright showers of water behind him.

For once they had left Toby at the house; they were on their way to the pa to make Mrs Lucy a present of part of the bacon, and Toby was always a nuisance there, trying to chase the dogs

They found the pa in a state of cheerful excitement. Before the steps of Mrs Lucy's house stood Luke's old red truck; it had a canopy over the back and from the canopy peered uncounted laughing faces. Just as the children arrived Mrs Lucy came out. She wore a rather grand black coat, and on her feet were white tennis shoes.

'We're going to the sports at Kauri Bay,' she announced. 'All the pa, almost. Luke is going to chop.'

'Wood-chopping,' she explained as the children's faces remained polite and blank. '*You* know. He's not bad at it.'

'Oh yes!' Callie said, light dawning. 'Oh, I do hope he wins!'

Mrs Lucy was very pleased with the bacon; sea water would not have harmed it, she said. She accepted also several pounds of squashed butter.

'I'm sorry it looks so funny,' Callie apologized.

'Will there be horses at the sports?' Jo asked a little wistfully.

'I guess,' said Mrs Lucy. 'They always have some jumping. Why don't you fellows come along with us? Plenty of room in the truck.'

'Oh . . . could we?' Jo gasped. They all took a step forwards and then the brightness went out of Miles's face. Callie stammered.

'It's . . . it's very kind of you, Mrs Lucy, we'd love to go, but I'm afraid we can't. We haven't brought any money with us.'

'Oh, money!' said Mrs Lucy royally. 'You can go in along with us. What you call a family ticket. Ten bob for the lot. Let's go.'

A great flurry followed. Someone passed up Rory, whose legs were too short to climb over the tailboard, and at the last minute they remembered Percy, and he was heaved up too. He had company, for there was already a hairy-faced puppy bedded down between two of the small children. Last of all Luke brought out his precious axes, and Mrs Lucy, carrying her grandson Hadley, Luke's youngest, climbed up next to the driver's seat.

'We're off!' she said. 'Anybody not here stays home!'

The truck bounced cheerfully up the track, and two other cars followed. They all sounded their horns and the journey had begun.

'Isn't it *fun*?' Jo whispered.

It was as well that the back of the truck was roomy, for it now contained several adults, uncounted children, Hadley's pram, a pile of water-melons and two dogs. Everyone settled down comfortably.

'I wish we'd put on tidier clothes,' Callie murmured. 'We're quite the worst-dressed people here.'

'Never mind, nobody will know who we are,' Jo said philosophically. 'They'll think we're some more of Mrs Lucy's grandchildren.'

This was taken as a tremendous joke by everyone in the back of the truck, and Manuel pointed an accusing finger at Jo's sun-bleached hair.

'That spoils it!' he said, which was taken as another very witty remark, and the pretty girl Rita, Luke's wife, patted Rory's sun-browned knees: 'This one looks enough like a Maori, anyway!'

Somebody passed round a bag of sweets; Rory and the smallest grandchild, Rosina, played with the puppy, the truck bounced and swayed on its way. All of a sudden, from out of the bush, they were passing through a small township and turning between fenced farm paddocks. The children, peering out from the canopy, saw rows of parked cars and all the cheerful bustle of people preparing to enjoy themselves.

'Oh look!' Jo cried rapturously. '*Horses!*'

'Keep your head down!' Callie hissed at her. 'Here . . . tie your scarf over your hair.'

Amid much giggling from everybody, Jo hastily untied the faded square from around her neck and draped it over her head. They could hear Mrs Lucy demanding from the gateman one family ticket.

'Looks like a blooming big family you've got back there!' he challenged her good-naturedly.

'Yes,' said Mrs Lucy in calm tones, 'I have been very fortunate.'

All of them, the gateman, Luke, Mrs Lucy herself, burst into delighted laughter, and the gateman, still laughing, motioned them in. The truck bumped over the grass. 'Good luck, Luke!' shouted a man trotting past on a shining chestnut mare.

'Same to you, mate!' Luke called back.

'Oh, isn't it beautiful?' Jo sighed.

Everyone unloaded themselves; and the pram was lifted down, and Hadley installed, very smart with his white frilled pillow and cover.

'May I push him?' Jo begged. 'We'll be awfully careful.'

Miles vanished in a few seconds with Manuel, and Jo and Callie made their way across the sunburned grass, pushing the pram, leading Percy on a long piece of flax and trying to keep track of Rory, who was rushing back and forth trying to see everything at once.

'Look, Callie!' he begged. 'There's going to be a tug-of-war!'

'Oh, the little ponies!' said Jo rapturously. 'We must go and watch.'

They spent a blissful hour watching the pony-jumping and light hunter class, and then Rory dragged them away to see the greasy pig chase. Amongst the crowd of men and boys Callie could see Miles and Manuel.

'Wouldn't it be wonderful if Miles caught it?' Jo said happily. 'Wouldn't you love to have a pig, Callie?'

'I don't know,' Callie said flatly. 'Where would we keep it?'

'Oh, we could make a pen,' Jo planned. 'Miles could make it.'

'Like the one he made for Amy,' Callie said unkindly. 'No, I don't think I want a pig. We'd never be able to have it killed.'

At that moment the pig was released and pandemonium broke loose. A small black galloping object streaked across the paddocks and, with shrieks and yells and wild thudding of feet, the pursuers tore after it; the onlookers cheered and shouted and urged them on, someone made a grab at the pig and its piercing screams were added to the uproar.

All this was too much for Percy; he barked and leaped upon his flax lead, which broke, and next minute Percy, Jo and Rory were added to the long train following the pig, while Callie, pushing Hadley, panted a very long way behind.

In a very short time Jo returned, dragging Rory by the hand and lamenting loudly.

'A big fat boy got the pig! Wasn't it a shame? It was the dearest little thing . . . and I did want a pig! And we've lost Percy!'

Percy seemed to have vanished. Jo was near to tears. 'What shall we do?'

'We'll find him,' Callie assured her, 'or he'll find us.'

They searched for ten minutes without success. It was Rory who finally located him. He tugged at Callie's arm.

'Look! Look! The police have got him!'

'What?' said Callie unbelievingly. 'Oh, don't be silly! What would the police want with Percy?'

Rory, however, was quite right. Percy was being led across the paddock by a tall man in blue shirt and dark trousers and a white helmet. When Percy saw the children he leaped and tugged on his lead, and the policeman let him go and he ran to them.

'Your dog?' he said to Callie, smiling as Percy knocked Rory flat with the force of his welcome.

'Yes,' Callie said, hurriedly gathering her manners. 'Thank you very much. We had lost him. I hope he wasn't doing any harm.'

'Only trying to get into cars. Looking for you, I expect.'

Callie felt that he was looking rather hard at them.

'I expect it was because he thought we were a funny mixture,' Jo said, when he had gone. 'You sounding so polite and all, and our old clothes and our little Maori baby. Don't you wish we had a baby, Callie?'

'I thought it was a pig you wanted,' Callie reminded her.

'Callie,' said Rory, 'I'm hungry, Callie. And there's a van over there selling hot pies.'

'Oh, Rory!' Callie protested. 'You promised you wouldn't say you were hungry. You know we haven't got any money.'

'Well, I'm thirsty then.' Rory's voice broke with self-pity.

At that moment Rosina appeared.

'My grandmother says you fellows are to come!' she announced.

They followed Rosina back to the truck, and there they found Mrs Lucy seated comfortably on the grass in the shade, with the members of her party in a circle around her. Before Mrs Lucy stood at least a dozen bottles of lemonade and raspberry drink, and a tremendous paper bag from which she was handing out hot meat pies.

'Come on, come on!' she called to the children. 'You're pretty slow. Somebody else will get your share.'

Rory did not need to be asked a second time; he sank on the grass beside her and took his pie in both hands.

'*Thank* you, Mrs Lucy!' he said as he bit into it.

Callie and Jo forgot their polite scruples and followed his example; the pies tasted delicious and the warm fizzy lemonade slid comfortingly down their parched throats. Manuel brought two of the water-melons from the truck and split them open with a blow from a big knife, and then cut them into thick slices.

They had scarcely finished the water-melons when Mrs Lucy said briskly: 'What's the time? Better get a move on, eh?'

Everything was hurriedly stowed in the truck. People were beginning to move in the direction of the enclosure where the chopping competitions were to take place. Mrs Lucy shepherded her party along and, with a little pushing, secured a place on the fence.

The six contestants for the underhand chop were setting up their logs. Number one, Manuel told the children, was Barry Bellman, the Waikato champion, a very big blond man with a self-satisfied air; then came Joe Chase, lean and dark and long-nosed, from Ninety Mile Beach; competitor three was Luke, fine and brown and handsome in his snowy white singlet and blue denims. Four and five were local men, and the last competitor was Barney Ohia, 'from up the bush', very broad, big and dark, older than the others, with a look of dignity about him.

'He is a real bushman,' Manuel said. 'Getting old now, but very good.'

The men moved about their positions, shifting their feet, feeling the edge of their axe blades, calling jokes to friends in the crowd. It was hot and the onlookers packed tightly around the fence; the judges waited; the men spat on their hands and gripped their axe handles.

Everyone had fallen silent, so that the small explosion of the starter's pistol made Callie jump. At once there rang out the clear sharp crack of the axes biting wood and the electrifying ripple of the falling chips. The onlookers began to roar. 'Come on, Luke!' someone bellowed in Callie's ear, almost deafening her. All about them people were yelling madly: 'Barry! Shake 'em up, Barry!' 'Come on, Joe!' And the children jumped and yelled too: 'Luke! Come on Luke!'

Through tears of excitement Callie saw the labouring men. The sun shone on Barry Bellman's great shoulders and the chips flew like bullets; his log was almost through. 'Oh no!' Callie wailed. Far down the line old Barney Ohia swung his axe unhurriedly, slowly it seemed in comparison with the others. Next instant Luke's log rolled apart.

A roar of cheering went up from the crowd; two seconds later old Barney's log was through; the Waikato champion followed him almost instantly. People ducked under the fence and rushed up to slap Luke on the back. A photographer ran across and pushed him into a victor's pose, axe in hand, foot on the fallen log, his handsome face split by a wide grin.

'Now he will be too conceited to live with!' Mrs Lucy said.

The presentation of Luke's cup was the climax of the day. He had been placed third in the standing chop, and the children had seen the young man on the chestnut mare win the open hunter event. The shadows were beginning to grow long and Mrs Lucy rounded up her party.

'Come on you, Luke,' she ordered, 'and no stopping

at the pubs on the way back either. Time we had all these kids home.'

Tired and sunburned and content, they all packed into the back of the dusty truck. Percy was tired too; he lay on Callie's feet and dreamed of pigs and policemen.

'I'm hungry!' Rory said.

'I knew you were going to say that!' Callie told him heartlessly. 'You'll just have to stay hungry till we get home.'

Callie was wrong, for as they passed through the township Luke stopped the truck and disappeared. He came back with a very large parcel wrapped in newspaper. When he opened it there arose the mouth-watering smell of fish and chips.

'Luke's shout,' Mrs Lucy announced, beginning to tear up the paper for plates, 'because he won. It's his shout for everybody.'

'Oh, thank you,' Callie murmured. 'It's very good of you, Mr Luke.'

Sitting in the back of the truck, eating fish and chips out of newspaper and finishing the last of the water-melons, Callie and Jo looked at each other and thought of Mrs Mac. Rory slid down and laid his head in Callie's lap and fell asleep.

'Hasn't everyone been kind to us?' Jo said drowsily as the truck bumped on its way again, 'and it's been the loveliest day. I just wish we had got that dear little pig.'

Chapter 13

'The discoveries . . . made me very eager
to see other parts of the coast.'
from *Robinson Crusoe*, by Daniel Defoe

It suddenly seemed to the children that the days were
slipping past with astonishing speed. Almost since they
had come to Penguin Island they had planned for their
great expedition up the coast, and now, early one cloud-
less morning, they made their last preparations for the
trip.

Callie packed provisions in her father's old rucksack,
and Miles took care of bait, fishing-lines and hooks; he
was to carry the rucksack, and Jo and Callie had the
sleeping-bags, rolled up and tied across their backs with
plaited flax. Rory carried the empty billy on a piece of flax.

They let the calf loose with Rosie, and Percy and the
kitten led the way, their tails waving happily.

'I suppose we'll be carrying her after a mile or two,'
Miles grumbled, trying to sound cross and not succeeding
very well.

It was a perfect morning, already hot. The sea was as smooth as glass, and away ahead of them the Cavallis were like ghost islands. Callie had a sensation of freedom that made her almost giddy. Nobody knew where they were going or where they would spend the night.

'We're like explorers,' she said. 'I feel as if we were going where nobody has ever been before.'

Once they had passed the stretch of tumbled rocks where the little blue penguins lived, the long sandy shore stretched before them, unmarked by human footprints. Only the oyster-catchers ran in front of them, ducking their heads and uttering long suspicious whistling cries. Jo wasted time following them, searching in the salt-whitened grass for a nest of late chicks.

'You're going the wrong way,' Miles told her impatiently. 'They run away from their nests, not towards them.'

'I know,' Jo sighed, 'Professor Gilroy's book said so, but I can't help hoping all the same.'

Only Miles wanted to make good time; the girls were content to drift along, paddling their feet in a tiny creek that flowed over the sand, picking up shells and pebbles, hanging entranced above a rock pool fringed with golden-green anemones. On a sally up into the sandhills Callie found a drift of native hibiscus, waist high stalky plants unfolding blooms of the purest sulphur-yellow, dark-centred, as big as teacups.

'They're the loveliest things I've ever seen,' Jo marvelled.

They walked until Rory complained that he was hungry, and then Callie shared out biscuits and cheese, and they drank water, cupped in their hands, from a spring that trickled out of the hillside. Percy lapped noisily and had his share of biscuits, but Toby had long since been asleep, tucked into the roll of Jo's sleeping-bag.

At midday they swam in a sheltered bay where the water was warm and so clear that they could see the shadows of small fish flickering away before them. Miles found fresh water and boiled the billy, and Callie built a fire of driftwood between two large flat stones. When the billy had boiled she produced sausages from the rucksack, and Miles cut and sharpened four green tea-tree sticks. Spitted on the sticks and roasted over the fire, the sausages were half raw and half burned, but nothing ever tasted better.

When the last morsel was gone the children put out the fire and curled up in the silvery sand in the shade and slept. Callie was the first to wake, and she lay there laughing to herself at the thought of how odd they would look if there was anybody to see them, like castaways on a desert island, wearing only faded bathing-suits, burned as brown as Maoris by the sun. Only Jo's long fair hair, bleached almost white by the sun, gave her away.

One by one the others awakened. Percy, stretched to his long length and panting loudly, opened his eyes, and Toby uncurled himself from Rory's neck. Miles was anxious to make a start. Callie had thought that Rory might be tired, but he was as anxious to be off as any of them. Even Toby was refreshed; she wanted to walk and trotted cheerfully along with her tail in the air.

'I'll catch a fish for you,' Rory promised her, and when they reached a stream mouth where the rocks shelved off steeply into deep water he insisted upon stopping and unpacking the fishing-lines.

Miles objected, but not very strongly, and he was soon happily occupied in baiting his line and Rory's. The two boys climbed out over the rocks, and Jo and Callie gathered pebbles from a cleft where they lay heaped like jewels, worn smooth by the action of the sea, glowing with colour.

'Look . . .' Jo gloated. 'It's like Mrs Mac's brooch, agate, all stripes, and the red ones must be jasper. Oh, Callie, let's take some back, perhaps some time we can get brooches or something made from them!'

They were so busy crouched over the pebbles, sorting them, that they were not watching the boys, and the first thing Callie heard was a great splashing and flapping. She sprang up and saw Miles dancing triumphantly on the rocks, pulling in a big silvery fish. Next minute his foot slipped and he plunged head first into deep water.

It all happened very quickly. One minute they were shouting with laughter at Miles's sudden ducking, watching him as he turned to swim back to the rocks; next minute Callie realized that he was making no headway, the run of the current was carrying him away from the point, to-ward the open sea.

Even as she ran, leaping over the tumbled rocks, she had a glimpse of his frightened face. She snatched Rory's fishing-line, wound on a heavy stick, ripped more line free and threw the stick with all her force. For a moment she thought it had fallen short and then she saw Miles make a splashing lunge towards it.

'Careful!' she shrieked at him. 'Don't jerk it. . . .'

For a moment it seemed impossible that the thin fishing-line could hold Miles's weight, but he kicked out sturdily, the gap of the few yards of swirling water narrowed, and next moment he had grabbed a ledge of overhanging rock and was scrambling out. His hands were cut and bleeding.

'What did you want to do that for?' Callie shouted at him in quite unreasonable rage.

'My foot slipped of course!' Miles yelled back. 'Anyone would think I did it on purpose!'

Callie sat down on a ledge of sun-warmed rock and began to shake. In those few moments, while Miles had struggled in the water, she had seen a cold and desolate picture of only three of them returning to the cottage at Penguin Island, only three of them to meet their father on his return. And she had promised him to look after the others.

Rory and Percy fishing

Jo, wide-eyed, and Miles, dripping water everywhere, stood by her, quite frightened, with no idea what to do. It was Rory who created a diversion. He gave a loud and piercing shriek, and they all rushed to the edge of the rocks to find him drawing in Miles's line with a very large and lively snapper still firmly on the hook.

'I've got a fish!' Rory was yelling. 'On Miles's line. It's a big one, look! Oooh! It's a big fish!'

'It really is a big one,' Miles said with satisfaction, rescuing it from the slippery rocks.

'Yes, and you're clever,' Callie told Rory, hugging him rather suddenly, so that he pushed her away.

'Miles and I,' he said loftily, 'we caught a big fish. There'll be enough for Toby.'

Miles cleaned and scaled the snapper and threaded a piece of flax through its gills, and added it to his load.

'That's going to get pretty heavy to carry,' Callie observed.

'Oh, I'll manage,' Miles said; 'but if we don't get going we'll never get anywhere near Lion Rock before tonight.'

They plodded on steadily for nearly two hours, but it had become apparent to them all that the headland they called Lion Rock was very much farther away than they had imagined. Callie was carrying Toby, and even Percy had stopped chasing seagulls.

'I'm hungry!' Rory said in a threatening voice.

'Can't we stop soon and camp?' Jo begged.

'I suppose so,' Miles allowed.

'The first nice place we come to then,' Callie agreed.

Quite suddenly they rounded a point and came into a little bay. Off shore stood tiny rock islands. The beach was fringed by gnarled pohutukawa trees, and above the beach was a tussocky terrace ringed about by more big trees. The white sand of the beach was reddened by fallen blossom.

Thankfully the children put down their packs, and Miles unsheathed his knife to cut the tussocky grass to make their beds. Callie and Jo gathered driftwood and built a fireplace. They had nothing in which to cook the fish, so they decided to wrap it in a length of kelp and cook it in the ashes of the fire as they had read that the old-time Maoris used to do. From a spring under the rocks they filled the billy and set it on to boil.

'Percy and I are going for a little walk,' Rory announced.

'I thought you'd had enough of walking,' Callie told him. 'Just a little way then, and don't go into the water. Dinner'll be ready soon.'

She watched him disappear behind the rocks, Percy at his heels, and then she sat down to wait for the fire to burn down to ash.

Waiting, she could almost have fallen asleep. Everything was very still, so that she could hear a grey warbler singing somewhere up the hill and the oyster-catchers at the end of the bay.

Suddenly Rory appeared coming down the beach. He shouted something so ridiculous that Callie was quite sure that she had heard him wrong.

'*What* did you say?' Miles yelled.

Rory stumped across the sand towards them. He looked quite placid and Percy trotted at his heels.

'I said,' Rory announced calmly, 'there's a dead man on the other side of the rocks.'

Chapter 14

'He was a comely handsome fellow, perfectly well made.'
from *Robinson Crusoe*, by Daniel Defoe

Nobody moved to go with Rory to look. They stood around in a little circle, quite close together.

'I don't believe a word of it,' Miles announced.

'You're just making it up!' Jo accused him tearfully.

Rory became a deep purple in the face and danced up and down in the sand, giving Percy a horrid fright.

'I'm not! I'm not! He's lying there all covered with sand! Go and look for yourselves!'

Miles took the lead and they filed slowly round the rocks. For some reason they went on tiptoe, as if afraid of waking the dead man. He lay curled in a drift of seaweed, wearing a red shirt and faded blue jeans wet with sea water. The ebbing tide had left his bare feet half buried in the sand.

All of a sudden everything seemed to Callie to be terribly lonely. They might have been at the end of the world. The sun had dipped behind the hills and the beach was in shadow. Spinifex heads rolled slowly at the margin of the waves, and a seagull wailed.

For a moment tears stung Callie's eyes. The dead man had fair hair and he looked very young, not such a great deal older than Miles, much too young to be dead on a summer night.

She dropped on her knees beside him fearfully. His eyes were closed and his face looked bruised, his hair matted with sand. With a great effort Callie reached out and touched his hand, and she gave a violent start.

The hand was cold, certainly, but not cold enough to be the hand of a dead man. She bent over quickly, and put her ear down beside his chest and could hear his heart beating.

'He's alive!' Jo screamed joyfully.

Her voice must have reached him, for his eyelids flickered. The four children knelt around him, and suddenly he opened his eyes. They were clear grey in colour. He looked from one to the other of the children quite blankly and wet his lips.

'Where am I?' he said thickly.

Callie looked at Miles and Miles looked at Jo. Nobody quite knew.

'We call that point over there Lion Rock,' Miles offered at last.

'We should try to get him along to the fire,' Callie said in an anxious whisper, 'Look, he's shivering . . .'

The boy opened his eyes again and then struggled up on one elbow. He rubbed a hand across his face bewilderedly.

'How did I *get* here?' he said in a despairing voice.

The children could not help him, for they knew no more than he did.

'Do you think you can get up?' Callie asked him

hesitatingly. 'I mean if we helped you? Our camp is only just behind the rocks there, and we have a fire, and you would get dry. Are you hurt anywhere?'

He tried to sit up, and groaned, and fell back again. With Callie and Miles helping him he made another effort and struggled up onto his feet and stood there swaying while they supported him.

'It's my head . . .' he muttered.

'Lean on us,' Callie encouraged him. 'It's not far.'

With much effort, guiding and supporting his staggering steps, they managed to reach the camp, and he sank down on one of the grass beds which Miles had prepared.

'He looks awfully ill,' Callie whispered, 'and he's so cold. Do you think you could get his wet clothes off, Miles? We haven't got anything he could wear, but he could get into your sleeping-bag, and we could dry his clothes by the fire.'

She put more sticks on the fire and brought the billy to the boil again and made tea. She carried a mug full, hot and strong and sweet, to the young man, now lying gratefully in Miles's sleeping-bag. He had a great blue bruise on one side of his head and his hair was matted with blood and sand. Callie had nothing to put on the wound, but she washed it carefully with hot water and bound it up with strips from her towel.

'Thank you very much,' the young man murmured. 'You are very good to me . . .'

'I'm so dreadfully hungry . . .' Rory complained unhappily.

Callie and Jo raked the seaweed parcel out of the ashes. So much had happened since Callie put it on to cook that she felt quite certain the fish would be cooked to a cinder. Instead it was done perfectly, the fish white and pearly.

She shared it out and sprinkled it with salt, and Jo buttered hunks of bread.

Toby and Percy had their share, but the young man ate only a mouthful and lay watching.

'I don't understand,' he said at last; 'where are the others?'

'What others . . . ?' Callie asked, bewildered. He must be delirious, she thought.

'Your parents . . . whoever you're with.'

'We are not with anybody,' Callie told him.

'You mean . . .' he said, his voice trailing off a little, 'that you children are away out here, wherever it is, miles from nowhere, on your own?'

'Not so much of the children!' Miles said, offended.

'Certainly,' Callie said in a haughty voice.

It seemed to make him worse thinking about it, for he held his head and groaned, and Callie asked him if he would like to try to sleep.

'We won't make a noise,' she promised, 'and we're going to bed ourselves directly we've finished eating.'

'But I can't keep the sleeping-bag,' he protested, rousing himself.

'Rory's sleeping-bag unzips,' Callie explained, 'and it's much too big for him anyway, so he and Miles can sleep under it quite well tonight. So long as you're warm.'

'Yes, thank you very much . . .' he said.

He hesitated, and Callie said:

'We should have told you who we are. Our name is Eliot and that is Miles, Jo and Rory. I'm Callie.'

'I'm sorry I can't tell you who I am,' he said, in a rather odd voice.

'Well, that's your business,' Callie said, after a second's pause. She sounded a little uncomfortable.

'No, you don't understand!' he said suddenly, pushing himself up on one elbow. '*I don't know what it is!* I don't know what I'm doing here, nor where I came from! I don't remember anything about myself at all!'

He looked so ill that the children were quite frightened.

'Oh, please don't think about it!' Callie begged. 'It must be that knock you had on your head. I'm sure you'll remember everything perfectly well when you wake up in the morning. Do please lie down now and try to sleep. . . .'

Callie was suddenly so tired that she could scarcely drag herself away from the fire. It had been a long day and a great deal had happened. She put sand on the ashes and crawled into her sleeping-bag. The others had settled down. Suddenly she was asleep.

It seemed a long night and yet a very short one. When she woke the sun was shining, and she felt almost as confused as their strange visitor. It took her a few seconds to remember where she was and what she was doing. She could see silvery grass stems, white sand and the pure, beautiful colour of the sea. She turned over and looked into a small tussocky field with over-arching trees and a winding stream. Under the trees there were a few rough-looking ponies grazing; one was an old white mare with a small dark foal.

She remembered slowly and sat up. There was a smell of wood smoke. Miles was already up and had a fire burning. The young man they had rescued sat beside him, dressed in his own clothes, bare-footed, his head still bandaged.

Callie scrambled out of her sleeping-bag and went down to the stream and washed her face, and wet and combed her hair. For some reason she was suddenly shy.

'Did you . . . ?' she began, when she came up to the fire. 'I mean, have you. . . ?'

He shook his head.

'No. I can't remember one single thing about myself before the moment when I woke up and you were all kneeling around looking at me.'

'Oh dear,' Callie said. 'But you do look better. Do you feel any better?'

He had a very nice face, she thought, even under the bandages. It was thin and brown with a steady look and good grey eyes.

'Yes, I do,' he said, 'a lot better. Only my head feels queer yet, and I seem to have done something to my foot. I can't put my weight on it.'

They looked at his ankle. It was swollen and bluish in colour.

'I hope it isn't broken or anything like that,' Callie said, worried. She began to wonder what they could possibly do with a man with a broken ankle, away out in the wilds, with no road near them.

The billy was boiling and Miles hooked it off the fire and put in the tea. They toasted the last of the bread, holding it on long sharp sticks. Callie had to shout to Jo to come and get her share; she was following the ponies around, watching them.

'Oh, the little foal!' she cried, forgetting to be shy as she sank down beside their visitor, 'It's so *sweet*! Do you like horses, Mr . . . what shall we call you?'

There was silence for a second or two and they looked at one another.

'Friday!' Miles cried suddenly. 'Like Robinson Crusoe, you know. Because yesterday was Friday, and we found you on the beach, just like Robinson Crusoe found Friday. . . .'

'We'll call you Friday,' Rory agreed, pointing a finger at him.

Everybody began to laugh. It was a very good thing, Callie thought, that Friday thought it funny too.

They had finished breakfast and she began gathering up the mugs to take them to the creek to wash them. She picked up the sheet of newspaper that had been wrapped round the bread. The date at the top was that of two days earlier; the bus driver had probably wrapped a spare newspaper round their groceries. Callie intended to save the sheet for starting a fire, but a headline caught her eye. She smoothed the paper out and went on reading.

'Armed Attack on Northland Bank,' the headline said. 'Teller injured by Masked Robber. Two men in the small bank agency at . . .' (this part of the paper was torn) 'held up yesterday by a masked man who escaped with the sum of about five thousand dollars in singles and five-dollar notes. The teller, Mr N. C. Taylor, made a plucky attempt to reach the bank revolver, but was shot and wounded in the shoulder and is now in hospital, where his condition is described as fair. The assailant is described as a young man, fair-haired, of slim build and wearing a red cotton shirt and blue denim trousers.'

Chapter 15

'The perturbation of my mind was very great.'
from *Robinson Crusoe*, by Daniel Defoe

It was not until afterwards that Callie realized that
the shock must have shown in her face. She wondered
why the others were all looking at her. Friday leaned
over and took the sheet of newspaper from her hand
and smoothed it out. Miles and Jo came to look over his
shoulder.

In books, Callie thought, people always turned as white
as sheets. Friday did not turn white; his tanned face was
a sickly grey. He laid the newspaper down and looked
from one to another of their faces.

'Oh, it can't be!' Callie cried sharply. 'Lots of people
wear red shirts and blue jeans! I don't see why you should
start imagining silly things like that. . . .'

Friday was unbuttoning the top of his shirt. He brought
out a small packet of greyish-looking paper and unfolded
it. It was a bundle of new, uncreased one-dollar notes,
still damp inside.

Pohutukawa trees by the shore

'Can you tell me where I got those?' he said in a low voice, 'and this . . . ?'

From the back pocket of his jeans he fetched out a small object which he laid down on the newspaper. Callie knew nothing about guns or ammunition, but she realized that it was a bullet of some kind.

She and Jo and Miles sat staring at it, silent. They drew together a little, and Rory came and leaned against her, uneasy, but not knowing why.

'The best thing you can do,' Friday said in a hard voice, 'is to get going. You don't want to get mixed up in all this. The less you have to do with me the better. Maybe I'm mad or something. Leave me here. I'll manage. Go home and forget you ever saw me.'

There was silence for a moment or two. Miles looked at Callie in protest. Jo was already beginning to cry. Callie's eyes met Friday's, and she made her decision swiftly.

'We're not going to leave you,' she said firmly. 'We

don't believe it, any of us, do we, Miles? You're not that sort of person. You can come back with us, nobody will see you, and you can stay until you're well and remember things again.'

She never knew what Friday would have said, for at that minute Rory tugged at her arm and pointed.

'Look!' he said. 'There's horses.'

There were two riders away up the beach, no sharper than shadows in the haze and spindrift.

'There's a place behind the rocks there,' Miles muttered, 'a sort of cave.'

They hustled Friday up onto his feet and helped him to limp into the shelter of the rocks. Miles took a branch and swept the sand clean of footprints, and they went back to the camp fire. Miles got out his fishing-gear and fiddled around with it, and Callie packed and unpacked the mugs.

'Don't you say anything to these people about Friday!' Callie warned Rory. 'In fact don't you say anything at all.'

It seemed to take a very long time for the riders to approach. By the time they arrived Callie's hands were trembling.

'Hallo!' the older man said to them. He looked as surprised as if they had been mermaids: 'What are you doing here?'

'We're breaking camp,' Callie told him very politely.

He was a big broad-shouldered man, riding a roan horse. His companion was dark and younger; he looked partly Maori.

'Where's your father?' the big man said. 'Or whoever you're with?'

Callie was getting tired of people asking them exactly that question.

'We're by ourselves,' she said. 'Can we do anything for you?'

'You mean,' he said, very much as Friday had done, 'you kids are camping out here on your own?'

'We're just having a picnic,' Callie told him.

'You haven't seen anything out of the way?' he asked them abruptly.

'Out of the way . . . ?' Callie repeated.

'Any wreckage, part of a small boat, anything like that? We're looking for a man who may have come this way.'

Callie shook her head and swallowed.

'We haven't seen any wreckage at all,' she said. 'Not up here.'

The big man shifted in his saddle and let one foot dangle out of the stirrup.

'Where are you from?' he asked. 'Which way did you come?'

It seemed to Callie it would be better to tell the truth.

'We walked up the beach,' she told. 'We're spending our holidays at Penguin Island.'

The man on the roan horse nodded thoughtfully.

'I guess we'll turn back here,' he said to his companion.

'Have you kids got a telephone?' he asked Callie.

'We can get to one,' Callie said.

He brought a pencil and notebook out of his pocket, scribbled something and tore the page out.

'That's the number. Give me a ring, will you, if you come across anything. Ask for Sergeant Dixon. Thanks.'

He picked up the reins, and the roan swung around and, in a moment, the two riders were cantering up the beach.

Miles and Callie stood looking after them.

'They were police, weren't they?' Miles said in a

half whisper. 'They must think that man got away in a
boat. . . .'

Callie nodded.

'But it's not Friday!' she said suddenly and almost
fiercely. 'I'm sure it's not Friday!'

They found Rory drawing pictures for Friday in the
smooth sand behind the rocks. They did not ask Friday
how much he had heard.

Suddenly he buried his head in his hands.

'Why can't I remember? I *must* remember. . . .'

'Oh, please don't!' Callie begged. 'I'm sure it's bad
for your head to try and remember. Try not to think
about it . . . it'll all come back to you when you're
better.'

'Maybe I don't want to remember,' Friday said, his
eyes closed and his face pale. 'Maybe that's what's the
matter with me.'

Miles and Callie drew away behind the rock and spoke
in whispers.

'What are we going to do? If only we could get him
home nobody would see him there, and he could lie quiet
till he's better.'

'He can't walk on that ankle,' Miles said, 'even if he
was well enough in other ways. Maybe two of us should
stay here with him, and the other two go back home for
things—food, blankets.'

'It would take so long,' Callie said, worried. 'Two
days. It would be much better if we could get him home.
Anyway . . . where's Jo?'

'Oh, somewhere around of course.'

Callie was looking quite frightened.

'So many things have happened, you nearly getting
drowned, us finding Friday, now if Jo's lost. . . .'

'Oh, don't be silly!' Miles exclaimed. 'She can't be lost.'

At that moment the bushes on the other side of the creek bed parted and Jo appeared. She was holding a knotted flax rope, and at the other end of the rope, following docilely, came the hollow-backed white mare. The dark little foal dodged nervously behind.

Jo's face was beaming with triumph.

'See!' she cried. 'She's as quiet as quiet. She didn't mind me catching her. And now Friday can *ride* home . . . isn't that a marvellous idea?'

Callie and Miles looked at each other.

'We can't steal a horse, foal and all!' Miles protested.

'It must belong to somebody,' Callie said. 'If it's quiet enough to let you catch it, somebody must ride it sometimes. We might be in worse trouble still if we just take it away. . . .'

'It's not *stealing*!' Jo cried. 'We wouldn't do such a thing! It would be just borrowing for a little while; we wouldn't do them any harm, we'd let them go directly we got home, and they could find their way back. There's no houses around, nothing for miles and miles, nobody would ever know!'

Callie made a helpless gesture. If they were already hiding a criminal from the police it was a very small matter to borrow a horse, but it made it all the more upsetting all the same.

'Friday! Friday!' Jo was calling happily. 'We've got a horse for you to ride now! You won't have to walk at all. . . . Isn't that wonderful?'

They gave Friday no chance at all to argue about whether he was coming home with them; they all four crowded round and insisted that he mount the white mare immediately. They had no idea how long it was since she had been ridden, but she made no objection when Miles helped Friday to scramble awkwardly astride. Jo had the very sensible idea of making flax stirrups from loops of flax hung across the mare's back to keep Friday's swollen foot from dangling.

So they set off on the way back to Penguin Island, Percy in the lead, ranging back and forth, and then Rory and the kitten; then came Jo, proudly leading the white mare, and behind trudged Miles and Callie. The little foal brought up the rear, plodding through the sand and rolling its eyes suspiciously.

Chapter 16

'Accordingly . . . I came home.'
from *Robinson Crusoe*, by Daniel Defoe

Callie thought that she would always afterwards have bad dreams about the journey home. The distance which they had covered so light-heartedly the day before seemed to stretch out for ever. The old white mare plodded very slowly, and Friday leaned over her shoulders, looking so ill that Callie thought he might at any time fall to the ground.

In the hottest part of the day they stopped and let Friday rest in the shade. Callie brought sea water and bathed his face. Miles fished doggedly and caught one small kahawai which Callie cooked and shared out. She gave most of her share to Rory, and Friday ate nothing, but drank thirstily of the hot, milkless tea.

'Next time we go on a trip,' Miles said grimly, 'we'll carry a lot more to eat.'

Darkness was falling when they finally forded the tide channel and plodded wearily up their own beach. Tears of sheer relief came into Callie's eyes at the sight of the little grey house tucked down in the sand hills, with the last light of evening reflected from its windows. Jo led the white mare up to the steps, and Friday slid off and fell sprawling in the sand.

'I'm all right,' he muttered to the frightened children, 'just stiff I guess, and my head aches. . . .'

'If you can just manage to get up the steps,' Callie said anxiously. 'Miles, can you take his other arm . . .'

They were all whispering, though there was nobody to hear. Jo hurried ahead and lighted a candle, and Friday stumbled up the steps and fell thankfully on the sofa. Jo ran for a blanket to cover him, and Callie hastily set a match to kindling and went out to fill the kettle.

'He looks awfully sick,' she whispered to Jo. 'I think we ought to try and get a doctor. . . .'

'Oh, no!' Jo said, frightened. 'No, we couldn't do that.'

In the other room Rory was already asleep on the rug by the fire, sitting up, his cheek on the cushion of the old wicker chair.

'I feel as if we'd been away for days and days,' Miles said.

'Try to drink something,' Callie begged of Friday when the kettle had boiled and she had made tea.

Friday sat up and drank thirstily and let Callie refill his cup.

'Don't worry about me,' he said. 'I'll be fine in the morning.'

Callie woke Rory and gave him a mug of tea and led him, staggering with sleep, to his bed. In a few moments, thankfully, she crawled into her own. Outside somewhere were a stolen mare and foal; in the next room was a man who might quite easily be violent and dangerous and was, in any case, wanted by the police. Callie was too tired to worry about any of it.

When she woke the sun was high in the sky. Suddenly anxious, she got up and dressed. She found Friday awake, propped up on the old sofa. His eyes were clear and he no longer looked feverish.

'Oh, you look better!' she said thankfully. 'Do you . . . ?

'Remember?' said Friday. 'No, not a thing.'

He threw back the rug and sat up.

'But I do know that I'm not staying here. Somebody will wonder what a stranger's doing here, then you'll be in trouble too. . . .'

'There's nobody to wonder.'

'Neighbours . . .' he began, but Callie opened the door.

'Have a look for them.'

He rose cautiously to his feet and limped over to the doorway, where he stood with Callie, looking out on the sand dunes, the lonely beach and the pale dazzle of the tide-flats. There was no sound but for the distant conversation of the oyster-catchers at the far end of the beach.

He blinked. 'Where are we?'

'We call it Penguin Island,' Callie offered.

Friday rubbed his eyes as if he scarcely believed them.

'You mean . . . you children are living by yourselves in this . . . this god-forsaken place. . . .'

'It's not a god-forsaken place!' Callie cried indignantly.

'I'm sorry,' Friday said. 'I don't mean it isn't beautiful.'

'And stop referring to me as a child!' Callie said huffily.

'I'm sorry,' Friday said again. 'But you do look very young. . . .'

'How old are you, Friday?' asked Rory, appearing.

'Don't worry him,' Callie said, 'and that reminds me . . .'

She went into the bedroom and delved in the trunk and brought out a grey shirt and a pair of her father's old shorts. She took them to Friday.

'I'm afraid they're a bit big,' she apologized, 'but if you put them on I could get rid of the red shirt.'

She went outside, and in a safe place on the sand she started a fire. When she came back Friday was wearing the grey shirt and shorts. The red shirt and jeans were rolled together, and she gathered them up.

'What about the money?' she asked.

'You can burn that too,' Friday said in a hard voice.

Callie unbuttoned the flap of the red shirt pocket and took out the notes. After a minute she went over to the window, lifted the loose board and slipped the notes underneath.

'Nobody will ever find them there, and maybe they belong to you.'

'Maybe, maybe,' he said, closing his eyes.

When she came back after putting the salt-stained jeans and the shirt on the fire, Friday was sitting with his head in his hands.

'Callie, I must get out of here. It's not just the police, but if I could try to kill a man I must be mad or something. I'm not the sort of person to be here with you and the children. I might do you some harm.'

Callie sat down on the foot of the sofa.

'I don't believe you're that sort of person!' she said flatly.

Friday leaned over and took both her hands in his.

'Look at me and tell me truthfully. Do you believe I did that?'

Callie looked back at him steadily.

'No!' she said. 'No, I don't believe it!'

'But the red shirt!' Friday said despairingly. 'The new notes!'

'I don't believe it,' Callie said, 'because I have feelings about people. And I know you're not that sort of person.'

Friday stared back at her with something like hope in his face.

'Please, Friday,' Callie said, 'give yourself a few days. Believe that you had nothing to do with it. You're not well enough to do anything just now. Stay here quietly, nobody will see you. Just don't think about anything. Then you'll remember, and *know* it's all right.'

'If only you could be right,' Friday said with a long sigh.

At that moment Jo came out.

'Oh, you're better!' she said, delighted, 'How nice! Would you like to come and see me milk Rosie?'

'No,' Callie said. 'He's got concussion, he's got to lie quiet.'

'What's that awful smell of burning?' Jo asked, wrinkling her nose. 'Callie, do you know that the horses are still here?'

'Oh no!' Callie said, horrified.

'Nobody will know that they had anything to do with Friday.'

'No, but it's *stealing*!' Callie said.

'You've got different clothes on!' Rory accused Friday.

'So that was the smell of burning,' said Miles. 'Good idea.'

Friday began to laugh suddenly and held his head in his hands. Rory came up to the side of the sofa and stared at him solemnly.

'What are you laughing at?' Jo begged.

'I think it's because you all sound so matter-of-fact . . . and so criminal,' Friday admitted.

'It is rather funny,' Callie said thoughtfully. 'I mean, up till a few weeks ago we never noticed the police, they were just like everybody else, as you might say. And since then . . .'

'You surprise me,' said Friday gravely.

'Oh, we haven't done anything *wrong*,' Callie assured him hurriedly. 'We'll tell you the story some time, but it's a very long one!'

'I'm hungry!' said Rory.

They ate the very last of the stale bread, toasted, and then Callie walked over the hill to get the order from the bus. Mrs Lucy called her to have a cup of tea and gave her a kitful of fresh silver-beet.

'One more in the house and you eat more,' she said wisely.

Callie stared at her vacantly and then closed her mouth. There seemed to be no point in arguing about it.

'Yes,' she said.

'How could she possibly know?' she demanded in a whisper of Jo and Miles directly she got home. 'Nobody's been over here. . . .'

Friday was sitting on the veranda; he had had enough of bed, he said.

'Will you be well enough to go out tomorrow?' Jo begged. 'We want to show you all our favourite places.'

'We can't drag him around miles on that bad ankle,' Callie warned.

'What about the boat you've got out the back there?' Friday asked.

'We've never had it out,' Miles confessed. 'It was too heavy for us to get it out of the shed.'

Stilts on the beach at Penguin Island

'And besides, Callie wouldn't let us,' Jo added. 'She said it had cracks in it and we'd all drown.'

'Very sensible,' Friday agreed. 'I expect the seams are opened up, being so long out of the water.'

They all trooped round to the shed, and Friday searched for a few minutes and produced two round, smooth spars.

'Rollers and all,' he said. 'Now we shan't be long.'

He showed them how to tilt up the bow of the boat and slide one roller underneath, and then push the boat forward onto the second.

'How easy a thing is when you know how!' Callie said as Friday moved the first roller ahead again.

Once in the water the boat promptly sank.

'It'll take up a bit by morning,' Friday said.

'Could we really use it?' Callie said doubtfully.

'Not to go to sea! But maybe I could get it seaworthy enough to pull out into the channel to fish, go across the estuary, maybe.'

'Oh, could we go across the estuary?' Jo begged. 'Manuel says there's a waterfall . . . we've always wanted to go.'

'We'll see,' Friday said.

'Oh, we do have fun!' Jo sighed. 'Oh, Friday, I do wish you would live with us for always!'

Chapter 17

'I was greatly delighted with my new companion.'
from *Robinson Crusoe*, by Daniel Defoe

The morning was very warm, still and calm. Callie had the strange sensation that everything was too beautiful to last. A peak spring tide brimmed the beaches.

Friday and Miles were already at work on the boat, packing the seams carefully with some old shredded rope they had found in the shed.

'It's not so bad,' Friday said. 'It's taken up quite a bit in the water. I guess we'd get across the estuary before it sank.'

Filled with energy the girls raced inside to make a hurried breakfast and pack up provisions for the day. They boiled eggs and cut a great pile of bread and butter, and packed up the billy with tea and sugar and cups. Jo milked Rosie and they wrapped a bottle of milk in wet newspaper.

'We'd better take the old pot to cook fish,' Callie said, 'or pipis.'

At last Friday announced that the boat was ready.

'I guess we can bail faster than she fills. Can you find a couple of tins, Callie? And did you say something about having one oar?'

'I never knew you could row with one oar,' Jo objected.

He took the oar and turned it over, looking at the name *Sandpiper* cut into the battered haft.

'For a moment . . . I almost feel as if I'd seen it before. . . .'

'We found it on the beach,' Callie said eagerly. 'Do you think . . .'

He shook his head. 'Whatever it is, it's gone now. Come on, load up, we're on our way.'

Callie waded out with the picnic gear, Jo hurled their bathing-suits aboard and Rory came carrying his kitten.

'Oh *no*!' said Miles.

'Oh *yes*!' said Rory, and Friday picked him up, kitten and all, and swung him into the boat.

'Toby likes going out in boats,' Rory announced.

Percy was last to come aboard. He plunged into the water with a howl, eyes rolling and ears flapping. He seemed quite convinced that the children were going to their deaths and had decided to go with them. Miles had to get into the water and hoist him from behind, and he scrambled awkwardly over the bow and fell on top of Toby and was rather badly scratched.

When the commotion had died down Friday took his place in the boat, dipped the single oar in the water and, with a waggling motion of the blade, propelled the little boat deftly into the tide.

'Oh, how clever!' Jo cried admiringly.

'Is it the Japanese who row like that?' Callie asked.

'Why do you suppose,' Miles said thoughtfully, 'that

you can remember how to do really difficult things, and yet you can't remember . . .'

'My own name!' said Friday, bursting into sudden laughter.

There was something different about Friday, Callie thought. It was as if he had made up his mind about something. The boat drifted on slowly; the sun was hot, and the water still and bright. Wisps of green seaweed and drifts of bubbles passed by on the turning tide. Callie, looking down, could see through the clear water to the sand and shells and pebbles of the sea floor.

'Isn't it beautiful . . . ?' she said dreamily.

'One thing you must promise me,' Friday said, suddenly sober. 'Never take this boat out by yourselves. It's not seaworthy for one thing, and, for another, you might get caught by the outgoing tide.'

'Oh no, we wouldn't,' Callie said. 'We promise that.'

'Anyway,' Jo coaxed, 'you'll be with us for a long time, Friday.'

Miles had already baited a hook and cast it over. He and Rory watched. Nobody seemed to notice that Friday had not answered.

'Where are we going to land?' Jo begged. 'See that lovely little beach where all the ferns are? Can we land there?'

Friday guided the boat through the shallows. They were coming into a beach where a small stream cut a blue path through the sand. Behind rose a green wall of bush fringed by sweeping tree ferns. Beside the stream, as in a Japanese painting, stood three great boulders.

The nose of the boat grounded and Percy was the first to leap ashore. The others followed him, carrying the picnic gear, the bathing-suits and towels and Toby. Callie stopped suddenly.

'Listen!' she said.

They heard the voices of birds and, as a background, the silvery sound of falling water.

'It's Manuel's waterfall!' Jo cried.

They followed the stream and it opened out into a sunny pool, ringed about by great boulders and fringed by ferns. From the bush high above them a narrow stream of water fell in a mist of spray.

'I want to swim!' Rory said, and in a few minutes they were all in the water, frolicking and ducking under the spray of the fall, and playing with Percy, who capered and barked and shook water over everyone. Only Toby sat disdainfully at the edge of the pool, washing her whiskers.

'It's like a pool in a fairy story,' Jo said, entranced.

'Yes, where the king's daughters come down to bathe every morning,' Friday agreed solemnly.

'And Callie and I are the princesses,' Jo said, giggling delightedly. 'Look, Callie, we're not much like princesses, are we?'

They bent over to look at their own reflections in the margin of the pool. Callie saw a thin girl with dark hair hanging wet over her shoulders, a girl burned as dark as a Maori, bare-legged in a faded bathing-suit.

'Only in disguise . . .' she said ruefully.

Miles had baited his lines and trudged off across the flats to the channel. He had to go a long way; Callie thought she had never seen the tide recede as far. Long, long stretches of grey sand and green weed glistened in the sunshine. She suggested to the others that they should walk out towards the ocean beach and dig for pipis.

'Otherwise there's only boiled eggs for lunch,' she reminded them.

They were digging unsuccessfully, and Rory was begin-

ning to complain that he was hungry when Callie heard
Friday shout. He was much farther out in the water than
the rest of them, well above his waist, and he had something in either hand.

'Bring the bucket!' he yelled. 'Quick!'

Callie ran, splashing through the water, and he tossed
two large shells into the bucket and dived out of sight.

'What are they?' Callie shrieked.

'Scallops! Hi! Here's another . . . oh, darn, he got
away! Here, quick, Callie!'

The excitement spread, and in a few seconds they were
all doubled up in the water, pawing madly, nearly drowning themselves. Miles had left his fishing and was rushing
to see what was happening.

'I've got one!' Jo screamed, 'No, it's gone . . . yes, I
have!'

The big shellfish were amazingly agile and speedy. Rory
actually captured one that had escaped to the shallows, and
he had to be rescued, spitting sea water, but clinging to
his precious scallop. All the screaming and excitement
were too much for Percy, who rushed in and out of the
water, barking hysterically and trying to rescue everybody
in turn. At last, quite weak with exertion and laughter,
they all waded out and fell down on the sand to gloat over
the bucket of handsome shells.

'They go so fast!' Jo complained, 'like fish!'

'They open and shut their shells,' Friday explained,
'and drive out the water. It's a kind of jet-propulsion!'

'Well, after all that . . .' said Callie, 'can you eat them?'

'Can you eat them?' said Friday pityingly. 'Poor ig-
norant girl. . . .'

They trudged back to their camp by the waterfall, and
Friday showed Miles how to open the shells with a knife.

'Oh dear!' Jo said. 'Do you eat that nasty hairy stuff?'

'No, you cut the beard off. There's the part you eat, inside.'

Callie left them to it, and she gathered wood and lighted a fire. For their table she chose a flat slab of rock set in silvery sand, and she laid out plates and mugs, bread and butter and eggs and salt. Friday announced that he would cook the scallops; he put them into the old iron pot, washed them in sea water, and then put the pot over the hot embers with a big lump of butter and a sprinkling of salt. Every few seconds he shook the pot.

'Come and get it!' he called and ladled out the scallops.

For quite a long time everybody was too busy to speak.

'That was a very nice dinner,' Rory said at last.

'It was super,' Jo said with her mouth still full. 'You are clever, Friday, there's so many things you can do . . . and you can teach us.'

'Let's climb to the top of the waterfall,' Callie suggested.

'I want to fish off the rocks when the tide turns,' Miles said.

'Let's go get more scallops,' Rory demanded.

'Let us just sit here in the nice cool shade,' Friday groaned.

In the end they did everything. They scrambled up through the bush and found a point where they could look down on the pool and its clouds of spray; they went out to channel and fished, and searched for the scallop bed, which seemed to have entirely disappeared.

When the tide moved in again towards the beach they went down reluctantly to push the boat out. The shadows were long.

'Oh, I wish we were just beginning the day!' Jo sighed.

'Where are your bathing togs?' Callie demanded of Rory.

She ran back up the stream and Friday followed her more slowly. The bathing-trunks were lying, damp and sandy and forgotten, on a stone by the water and, as Callie picked them up, she found Friday beside her.

'Oh, thank you, Friday,' she said. 'For the day, I mean. . . .'

'Yes, it's been a good day,' Friday said slowly.

Callie looked down at the bathing-trunks, faded and shrunken.

'It's had the feeling', she said, 'of a last day, some-how. . . .'

Friday nodded soberly.

'I knew you would understand, Callie, even if the others didn't. You know what I've got to do, don't you?'

Callie folded Rory's bathing trunks and unfolded them again.

'Yes, Friday.'

'I can't stay skulking here. I must go into a police station somewhere and give myself up, and *find out.*'

A pair of fantails, squeaking happily, flew over their heads and then fluttered between them, brushing their faces.

'When will you go?' asked Callie in a low voice.

'Tomorrow morning,' Friday said, 'first thing. I'll walk over and catch the morning bus.'

They walked silently down the beach.

'I know it will be all right, Friday!' Callie said urgently.

They bailed the water out of the boat and clambered aboard. Only Toby was missing; she refused to be caught and flew madly up and down the beach, her tail blown up and her whiskers twitching. It was the hour of the day when she always went crazy. The children coaxed and chased her, but she kept just out of reach and Rory was reduced almost to tears.

'We'll pretend we're going to leave her,' Friday suggested.

They climbed into the boat again and Friday drove it from the shore.

'Don't go too far!' Rory begged.

Looking back anxiously they saw a small pathetic black shape dash out of the bush and down to the water's edge.

'Go back, go back!' Rory wailed.

Toby was shaking her wet paws and shrieking piteously as Jo tumbled out of the boat and ran to pick her up. Once in the boat she sat alone and outraged, drying her paws and twitching her tail.

Slowly they drifted across the still water of the estuary with the gulls wheeling in a lazy pattern overhead. Away down the beach they could hear the distant voices of the oyster-catchers.

It was the hour when Toby always went crazy

Suddenly, ahead of them, the water parted and they saw a shining curve.

'It's Gabriel!' Jo cried. 'Look, Friday, look! It's our dolphin! We wanted you to see him more than anything!'

They all sat silent, watching.

'I think he comes when he hears our voices,' Callie whispered. 'He must have heard us calling Toby.'

Slowly Gabriel moved up alongside the boat, dived deeply down, and rose again. He was less than six feet distant; they could all see his glistening dark body, his blunt nose and bright wrinkled eye. Almost he seemed to look and smile at them.

'Hasn't he got the *nicest* face?' Jo said lovingly.

It was as if her voice had broken the enchantment. Gabriel turned suddenly, frolicked and dived, and then he was gone.

They landed and dragged the boat up on the sand. The day was over.

Chapter 18

'We expected that we all would have perished
immediately.'
from *Robinson Crusoe*, by Daniel Defoe

In the morning they all moved about quietly and a little
forlornly. The blue calm weather had suddenly vanished;
long feathery mares' tails of cloud swooped across the sky
and a high hot wind blew. Callie cooked eggs for breakfast and made a little packet of sandwiches for Friday.

'I thought you might get hungry on the bus,' she said.

'Thank you,' Friday said gravely. He was looking into
the glass fishing float that stood by the window-sill.

'Some people believe you can see the future if you look
in a crystal ball,' Jo said.

'Ah yes,' Friday said, 'but it's my past I want to see.'

'Can we walk over to the bus with you?' Jo begged.

'Better not,' Friday said. 'I don't want anyone to know
I've been here.'

Callie had found him an old razor of her father's and he
had shaved, but he was still bare-footed, and he limped a

little as he walked. He took Callie's sandwiches and the little packet of notes.

'It doesn't matter now,' he said.

They walked with him as far as the top of the hill. Percy and the kitten added themselves to the party. From the hill they looked back on the wind-whipped water and the little grey house by the beach.

'It was nice there,' Friday said. 'Well . . . goodbye.'

Jo had begun to cry bitterly. 'Goodbye, dear Friday,' she said, and Callie and Friday shook hands quite stiffly, like people who had only just met.

'I know it'll be all right,' Callie said, swallowing.

'Don't go!' said Rory in a gruff voice, but next moment Friday had turned away, and they watched his figure growing smaller as he walked down the rough track toward the road.

They trailed back to Penguin Island silently and soberly. The high hot wind made Callie feel restless.

'I wonder where Friday is now,' Jo mourned when they sat down to lunch.

'Let's go out this afternoon,' Callie said. 'The wind is too horrid for swimming; if we went over to the other side of the island it would be sheltered. Let's take our tea and go right down to the point.'

Callie made preparations as cheerfully as possible, but nobody was in very high spirits. They were climbing the hill path when Rory said in a solemn voice: 'It would be nice if Friday was here too.'

From the top of the hill, looking northwards, the long sweep of the coast was blurred with haze and flying sand from the off-shore wind.

'Doesn't it look queer?' Jo said. 'And there's smoke over the hill.'

'It's funny, isn't it,' Callie said, 'when you think we've been away up the beach there? Some day we'll go again.'

'That's where we found Friday,' Rory said.

They scrambled along the rough hillside path and made their way down into Gabriel's Bay. As usual they searched for treasure trove; Jo picked up a beautiful shell with tiger markings, and Miles collected some pieces of splintered timber which looked as if they might have come from a boat.

At the seaward end of the island the hills plunged down to a wild jumble of giant rocks. Between land and sea was a tiny cove with a narrow shelf of pebbly beach. At low tide a long line of rocks ran out, like a natural causeway, to a flat rock island swept by the waves.

The sun was low in the sky when they scrambled down to the narrow beach and began to gather firewood. Percy barked happily at a crab under the rocks. Callie had brought sausages, and, when the fire had burned down a little, they spitted them on long sticks and toasted them.

'I suppose we had better start back,' Callie sighed when they had eaten the last morsels and licked the grease from their fingers. 'We want to get up to the top of the hills, anyway, before dark.'

'How queer the light is!' Jo said, looking around her uneasily. 'It's sort of brown . . .'

In almost the same breath Callie said sharply: 'What's that noise?'

It was a muffled, crackling roar, quite different from the sound of the wind that blew above the sheltered beach. A sudden cloud of pungent smoke rolled down on the children and, as they sprang to their feet, they saw a terrifying sight. Above them, the whole hillside was on fire. From the dry scrub and flax bushes, flames sprang twenty feet into the air and, blown on the gale, swept down toward the narrow ledge of the beach with incredible fierceness and speed.

For a moment Callie felt that her knees had turned to water. She was quite unable to move. Rory's white face swam dizzily in her sight, and she forced herself into action, pushing the others with her.

'Quick!' she said hoarsely. 'Get out into the sea . . . along the rocks there. . . .'

'Toby!' Jo screamed. 'Where's Toby. . . ?'

She pursued the kitten round the rocks and snatched her up; Callie was dragging Rory by the hand. Percy was no trouble; he ran at their heels, whining unhappily as they stumbled over the wet slippery rocks where the water was beginning to cover the causeway.

'Right out to the end . . .' Callie panted. 'Lie down, put your heads down . . .'

They were choking and coughing in the swirling smoke; tears ran down their faces; the whole world had turned into a red terror of heat and thundering, crackling fire. Callie lay face downwards on the flat rock, her arm around Rory, and the spray blew over them; after a minute she tore off the scarf she had worn on her head and dipped it in the water and tied it over his nose and mouth. Jo and Miles crouched beside them, with Percy whimpering and huddling in terror. Burning pieces of fern fell around them and hissed in the water.

'I think perhaps the worst is over . . .' Callie said at last in a hoarse whisper.

They dared in time to sit up, their faces still turned away from the heat. Jo's teeth were chattering, and her face was smeared with ash. Miles had a burn on one hand and Percy's coat was singed by flying sparks. Callie dipped her scarf in the sea again and, in turn, they bathed their eyes. The smoke still swirled around them, thick and pungent. Tears ran silently down Rory's smudged cheeks.

'We're going to be all right,' Callie assured him. 'The fire'll go out soon. Look at Toby. . . .'

Jo had thrust the kitten down inside the neck of her jersey. Now Toby pushed her face up under Jo's chin and sneezed crossly. She did not like the smoke at all.

Rory managed a rather tearful giggle. Miles was looking very soberly at Callie, and Callie looked back. She was measuring with her eye the depth of the water already covering the natural causeway that was their only way back to shore. It would be quite a long time before the fire would cool enough for them to be able to go back to the beach. Callie was trying to remember whether the big flat rock that was their refuge was covered at high tide. Percy lifted his head and yawned nervously, and laid his jaw on Callie's knee. At that moment a big wave broke and splashed them with spray.

'I'm hungry!' Rory said defiantly.

'Oh, Rosie!' Jo broke out in a wail, 'and Freckles . . . what has happened to Rosie and Freckles? They'll be burned. . . .'

'I don't think so,' Callie said firmly. 'The wind was blowing this way, away from our bay, the fire was most likely not down that side at all.'

'Maybe the house is burned,' Miles said gruffly.

'It can't be helped,' Callie said. 'We're alive, and we might have been burned. We've got to thank God for that. And we've got to think about staying alive.'

'How soon can we get back to the beach?' Miles said.

'Not yet . . .' Callie said.

A clump of trees, slower-burning, had blazed up, and

the light fell red and glittering around them. The heat blew in their faces.

'The tide's coming in fast . . .' Miles warned, muttering.

The rocks leading to the shore were well submerged. A wave drove down over them and sent up a shower of spray which made Callie shudder. Even now, she thought, it would be impossible for them to reach the shore through the swirling surf; to be swept off the drowned causeway would be the end of everything.

'We'll stay here,' Callie said, trying to keep her teeth from chattering. 'Even if the tide comes in we can hang onto the rock, and to each other. . . .'

'I'm hungry . . .' Rory said, his voice shaking.

Callie felt in the pocket of her shorts and brought out two apples, very small and rather green. Miles produced his knife and cut each apple in half. They sat and chewed the pieces of apple, and before they were finished the first wave broke over their rock refuge, drenching them.

'We must all sit close together,' Callie said, trying to keep her voice calm, 'Then we can hold onto each other and onto the bit of rock that sticks up.'

She put her arm around Rory, and Miles sat close on his other hand. Jo huddled against Miles, holding Toby under her jersey. They were all shivering. Percy lay and shivered too.

It was almost dark now; only the red glow of the still-burning fires lighted the sea. The wind had fallen a little, but the waves sucked and crashed and swirled about the jagged rocks. Their white crests looked red in the firelight. The children clutched at the wet rock surface and at each other as a bigger breaker than the rest hurled a torrent of spray over them.

Under Jo's wet jersey the kitten wailed. Callie's teeth were chattering as she said: 'The tide won't stay in very long. It's just a matter of hanging on till it goes out again.'

In her own mind she knew that the tide was still far from full.

'Please God help us . . .' she prayed. 'I promised to look after the others. . . .'

'What's that?' said Jo's hoarse voice.

Miles's head had jerked up. They all listened.

'It's a boat!' Jo cried.

Now they could hear the beat of the engine quite plainly. It seemed as if the launch might be moving parallel with the shore, towards the point.

'Shout!' Callie cried desperately. 'All of us at once! As loud as you can. . . .'

They all screamed at the tops of their voices: 'Help! Help! Cooee!' The wind and the sea made their voices thin, snatched them away. The steady beat of the launch's engine kept on.

'Oh, if only we had something to make a noise . . .' Callie gasped. 'Percy, bark! Bark!' She seized him and shook him, but he only whined apologetically.

'Help! Help!' they screamed again.

At that moment a wave broke over the rock. For a moment Callie lost her hold; drenched, she clutched fiercely at Rory and at the rock. The water ebbed, and they could now see the light of the launch, moving away from them, turning to round the point.

'It's gone,' Jo said dully. 'They don't see us. . . .'

Callie never remembered afterwards what it was that made her turn her head. Off shore from them, in the red light of the dying fires, she saw a dark shape lift and curve gracefully through the waves.

'It's Gabriel . . .!' Callie cried, and the tears rose to her smarting eyes, and she became suddenly aware of Jo shaking her arm.

'Look . . . look, the boat's turning. . . .'

The light of the launch was swinging round. A big wave broke over the rock, buffeting them, but now, with a fierce hope, they clung to one another.

'They've seen us . . .' Miles said gruffly.

Swiftly the launch was bearing down on them, its engine beating steadily, spray flying from the bow. Anxiously the children watched while it veered slightly to approach on the sheltered side of the rocks. There were two men, one at the wheel, one waiting with a boat-hook and, as the boat turned, the reflected firelight showed their faces.

'It's Friday!' Jo screamed.

At the same moment Callie cried: 'Father! It's Father!'

It seemed so much like a miracle that nobody could believe it. For a moment the tossing boat was close beside them, anchored by Friday's boat-hook. Callie could see his face, stern and set, as she held Rory at the edge of the rock.

'Jump!' Friday shouted, and Rory jumped obediently, landing on hands and knees, but safely. The launch swung away in the backwash of a wave and began to circle again.

'Be ready!' Friday called, and then, next minute, '*Now!*'

They all jumped. Percy howled and jumped too, and fell just short. His claws scrabbled on the boat's stern. To Callie it all seemed to happen so slowly that she felt she was watching a picture in slow motion. At the moment John Eliot swung the boat away from the rock Friday grabbed for Percy and they were both flung overboard into the seething water.

Callie felt her scream dry in her throat. Her father was shouting at her from the wheel. 'The rope! Throw the rope, Callie!'

Madly Callie grabbed up the wet coils and flung them. For a moment Friday had disappeared, and then his head bobbed up dangerously near the rocks. He was swimming strongly and next minute he had caught the rope and was pulling himself back alongside. Percy appeared, paddling wildly, and Friday grabbed him by the back of the neck.

Hoisted from behind by Friday, pulled from above by Callie and Miles, Percy was dragged aboard, and Friday followed him and fell into a wet heap and coughed up salt water. When he could speak he said a very odd thing. He said:

'What on earth has happened to Professor Gilroy?'

Chapter 19

'Having thus settled our affairs.'
from *Robinson Crusoe*, by Daniel Defoe

'Of course,' said Friday, 'if it hadn't been for the dolphin. . . .'

The little grey house was still standing; Rosie and the calf, the old mare and the shy foal were grazing among the flax bushes; they had all escaped the fire which had raced through the scrub of the mainland hills, and leaped across the tide channel to burn from the spine of the island down the seaward slopes to the beach.

On the morning afterwards a number of people were gathered, trying to put the story together. Friday and Jo and Miles sat on the edge of the veranda; Callie was curled on the steps; in one sagging deck-chair sat John Eliot with Rory and the kitten draped over his knees, and in the other chair, opposite, with his long legs stretched out, was Professor Gilroy.

'If somebody would start at the beginning . . .' Callie said. She had slept confusedly, her night broken by bad dreams; even now she kept looking from one to the other to be sure that everyone was safe, Percy sat beside her and thumped his tail reassuringly.

'Well,' said Friday, 'shall I begin? It won't take long. When I got off the bus yesterday the first thing I did was to look for the police station, which is a little old building that looks as if it was put up during the Maori wars. I walked in, and there was a fellow sitting at a desk, reading a newspaper. He asked me what he could do for me, and I was just about to tell him when I saw the headlines spread across the paper.

'They went something like "Attacker of bank teller captured. Youth confesses to shooting. Traced by numbers on notes."

'"What's up with you?" the sergeant said to me. "You don't look too good. Better sit down. I'll tell Joe to make us some coffee."

'Well I guess that must have been one of the best moments of my life. I didn't care any more who I was, I knew who I wasn't. We sat and drank the coffee and I told the sergeant the story, but he couldn't help me. He didn't know who I was, and the only thing he could tell me was that there'd been some wreckage washed up on the beach, and they'd had a search, thinking there might be survivors.'

'Those must have been the two men on horses we saw,' Callie said.

'When we made you hide in the cave,' Jo reminded Friday. 'What are you laughing at?' she demanded suspiciously of her father.

'Nothing,' John Eliot said. 'Let Chris go on.'

'Well,' Friday resumed, 'the sergeant then made a very funny remark. He said: "Now, if you'd been four children. . . ." So I pricked up my ears. "What do you mean, if I'd been four children?" I asked him. "Well," he said, "I just had a man in here—there he is, going down to the wharf now—saying he's lost four children. I've got a very good idea I've seen them around, but I'm damned if I know where they are now." And now I think it's your father's turn. . . .'

'You begin at the beginning too,' Jo begged.

'Well,' John Eliot began obediently, 'it was really that letter of yours. It seemed odd to me. For one thing, Rory's kitten. Had you forgotten that cats give Aunt Irene asthma?'

'I did know,' Callie said ruefully. 'I'd forgotten.'

'We were so busy at the time that I really didn't get around to worrying about it. When I had more time I couldn't get it out of my mind, then I had a letter from poor old Aunt Irene, written from hospital, telling me about her accident, not a word of you.'

'But we didn't want you to come back!' Callie lamented. 'That's why we wouldn't tell you. We were perfectly all right.'

'I'd done what I went down to do,' her father said. 'I'd got all the data and photographic material; it's just a matter of writing up, which I can do just as well from here. There was a plane coming back and I had no trouble getting permission to come.'

'And then you went to see Aunt Irene,' Callie prompted. 'I'm so glad she's getting better. We've been horrid, we hardly thought of her.'

'Let Father get on with the story, can't you?' Miles objected.

'So then I flew to Auckland. Theo McKenzie didn't know anything of you, and Mrs Mac is still in Scotland.

The woman at the boarding-house swore you'd said you were going to stay with cousins in the South Island. The only relations I could think of were the Rogersons; you know, my cousin Jan who married Jim Rogerson, they live in Queenstown.'

'We thought their name was Robertson,' Callie said, giggling.

'So I rang them and drew another blank. I'd lost a whole family, four children, disappeared into thin air.'

'When did you think of Penguin Island?' Jo begged.

'It was only a faint idea. I got Road Services to look up the passenger list for that day, but there were no Eliots.'

'We called ourselves Taylor,' Jo said with satisfaction.

'Yes, and gave me a lot more trouble,' John Eliot said without anger, 'but just why, may I ask?'

'Well, there were the police, you see . . .' Jo said obscurely.

'She said she was going to send for the police,' Miles explained, 'that Mrs Green, the boarding-house woman, because she wasn't going to have four children left on her hands.'

'So when we saw the police car outside,' Callie said, 'we climbed down the fire escape and went to the bus office and said our name was Taylor. Now I come to think of it,' she added, 'the police had probably come for something else altogether, and had never heard of us.'

'You see what a guilty conscience can do,' her father said gravely.

'And then?' Jo prompted.

'And then I decided to follow my hunch and come up here. If I hadn't found you then I was going to the police to get a general call put out. In fact I went to the police

station, and the sergeant was pretty sure it was you he'd
seen at the sports a while back, and again on the beach one
day, but he didn't know where you'd come from. So I
decided to go down to the wharf and hire a boat; I asked
old Bill if he'd taken you round to the island before Christmas, and he said no, and just at that minute a young man
came up to me and said: "Excuse me, are you the man
that's lost four children?"'

'And it was Friday!' Rory said, delighted.

'Chris Finlayson,' Jo said. 'It's a nice name, isn't it?'

'Do keep quiet and let Father get on!' Miles said
impatiently.

'So then', his father said, 'we joined forces. I took one
of old Bill's boats, and we got some stores and started off
for the island. On the way Chris told me his part of the
story. It was just dusk when we saw the fire and we didn't
like the look of it at all. We'd no way of telling if it was
burning on the other side of the island, but we put on all
the speed we could. We were just rounding the point
when we saw the lights of another boat.'

'That was Paul,' said Rory, making the matter clear,
'and Manuel, they came down the river in their boat to
look for us because of the fire. Mrs Lucy sent them.'

'Yes, well,' John Eliot said, 'naturally we were looking
that way and we never saw you on the rocks or heard you
calling. Only suddenly something caught Chris's eye and
he looked back and in the reflection from the fires he
saw your dolphin jump.'

'And then you looked back and saw us,' Rory said,
satisfied.

'Darling Gabriel!' said Jo, ready to weep. 'He must
have come because he heard us shouting. And he saved
our lives, didn't he?'

'Tell us how you remembered,' Miles begged of Friday.

'Well . . .' Friday said slowly. 'It was when I fell into the water. Suddenly it seemed to me I'd done all this before. I remembered being thrown on to the rocks when *Sandpiper* struck, and I thought of Professor Gilroy, marooned by himself on Castle Rock, with nothing to eat!'

Professor Gilroy uncrossed his long legs.

'You exaggerate, my dear boy,' he said. 'It was very annoying for me, running out of film, and I admit I was very worried about you, but I assure you nobody could be short of food on a sea island. There were many kinds of edible seaweed, beside shellfish, even if I had been unable to catch fish on a hand-line. Besides, I still had some of that goats' meat we salted after our shooting expedition.'

'So now I remember why I had that bullet in my pocket!'

'And the new dollar notes?' Callie asked. 'Why were they all new?'

'I'm afraid that was my fault,' the Professor said apologetically. 'I like to have plenty of cash with me, so I cashed a rather large cheque at the bank before I left, and asked for small notes, and they gave me all new ones. And when Chris went for provisions I gave him a bundle.'

'And a lot of worry,' Friday said.

'Nothing to the worry you gave me!' said Professor Gilroy.

'We seem to keep on interrupting you,' Callie said, 'but how long had you been on this island, and why did you go there?'

'To photograph birds of course.' Professor Gilroy seemed surprised that there could be any question. 'I wanted someone who could handle boats, and I asked Chris if he would like to spend his university vacation with me, and do a bit of exploring around the Cavallis and some of the little-known islands. We'd been on Castle Rock a week when the storm blew up. I must admit,' he added, 'that the force of the wind and sea quite took us by surprise. We had the dinghy beached where we thought it would be safe, but the waves damaged it and we lost an oar. Also our store tent was blown into the sea and we lost provisions and unused film.'

'And we ate your bacon,' said Rory, smiling angelically. 'Us and Mrs Lucy.' And they all burst into laughter.

'And then we had trouble with *Sandpiper*'s engine,' Friday said, continuing the story. 'I thought I had her right when I set off for stores, but she cut out, and the set of the current piled her up on the rocks. That's the last thing I remember until I woke up on the beach with the four of you standing round looking at me.'

'And then you didn't remember anything at all,' Jo said.

'And then the two policemen came and we hid you,' Callie said ruefully. 'We do seem to have been very silly.'

'And you rode the horse home,' Rory added his bit to the story.

'Oh, Father!' Callie said, 'the mare and foal are still here; they won't go home. Could we find out whose they are and buy them?'

'Oh, please!' Jo chimed in. 'The foal is so sweet. Please, Father! It would grow up and be very useful.'

'I must confess', said Professor Gilroy thoughtfully, 'that I have mostly thought of that type of amnesia, or loss of memory, as more or less an invention of female novelists. But I believe it can quite frequently be a symptom of concussion, and I should imagine it was the shock of Chris's fall overboard last night, almost repeating his first accident, that restored his memory to him.'

'Do you mind if we go on calling you Friday?' Jo asked.

'Not at all,' Friday said. 'I rather like it.'

There was a sudden commotion of barking dogs. Toby blew up to twice her size; Percy leaped up and added his voice to the din.

'It's Mrs Lucy!' cried Rory triumphantly.

It was Mrs Lucy indeed, her long black skirts bunched up, and seated in very queenly fashion astride the saddle of a large piebald mare with a rolling eye. She was attended by half a dozen dogs and by Manuel, trailing some distance behind and mounted on a dun-coloured pony.

John Eliot went quickly to the piebald mare's head and helped Mrs Lucy to dismount. She took both his hands in hers.

'My old friend John,' she said. 'It's good to see you again.'

'You've been very good to my children. I'll never be able to thank you.'

Callie and Jo hurried inside to put the kettle on.

'Eight . . . nine people!' Jo said. 'Like a party . . . isn't it fun? And there's all that cake and stuff Friday brought . . . there's not enough cups, we'll have to use the picnic mugs. Oh, isn't it wonderful that darling Rosie and the calf are all right?'

Friday had come through to help set out the cups and saucers.

'Funny,' he said to Callie, 'you look different today. Older than you did with shorts and bare feet.'

'I'm growing older,' Callie sighed. 'Older than when we came here, I mean.'

'But we've had a wonderful time, haven't we, Callie?' Jo begged, 'and we'll come back again every year, like we used to, Father says so. . . .'

'Yes, we've had a wonderful time,' Callie said, 'and it's almost over. . . .'

'You'll come back too,' Jo beseeched Friday. 'You will, won't you? Promise us. . . .'

'Yes, I promise you,' Friday said. He was answering Jo, but it was Callie he was looking at, smilingly and steadily. 'I'll come back again. I promise you. When you're a little older.'